Zachary Babington

Advice to Grand Jurors in Cases of Blood

Asserting from law and reason

Zachary Babington

Advice to Grand Jurors in Cases of Blood
Asserting from law and reason

ISBN/EAN: 9783337393137

Printed in Europe, USA, Canada, Australia, Japan

Cover: Foto ©Andreas Hilbeck / pixelio.de

More available books at **www.hansebooks.com**

THE
AUTHOR
TO THE
Reader.

 E that reads the
enſuing Tract, will
ſoon find that much
of the beginning of
it is by way of In-
troduction to the Subject-matter

of

of the Book, and might well (if
not better) have paſt under the
Title of A Preface, and therefore might have excuſed this: in
which I ſhall endeavour to ſhew
the Grounds and Reaſons that
put me upon this Argument; an-
ſwering all Objections that may
be made againſt the Author, for
being a Sanguinary Perſon, in
treating ſo poſitively upon this
Subject; ſhew the neceſſity of de-
termining the Law herein, in
point of practice by Grand Jurors in Caſes of Blood; give ſome
ſatisfaction to ſuch as may ob-
ject againſt the length of it,
whereas the Queſtion is ſo ſhort;
explain the Grand Jurors Oath;
and laſtly, endeavour to remove
all Difficulties made by them upon the ſaid Oath.

Two Reaſons principally moved me to this Undertaking;
The one was, The great Conteſts
and Differences I have too often obſerved between the Judges
and Grand Jurors about finding
of

*of Bills in Cases of Blood,
whereby the whole matter of
Fact, with all its Circumstances,
might receive its full disquisition in Court, and not in a* Grand
Juries *Chamber;* the Grand Jurors (*as if they were Judges
both of the Law and the Fact,
which is sufficiently demonstra-
ted in the ensuing Discourse they
are of neither*) *finding the Indictment sometimes Manslaughter,
when they should find it Murther, contrary to the sense and
direction of the Learned Judge,
and of the King's Council, whereby a Murtherer many times e-
scapes.*

*The second Reason was, That
if the Law were not determined in this point, betwixt the*
Judges *and* Grand Jurors, *the
Consequence must needs be, That*
Grand Jurors (*that hear but one
side*) *would in the end take the
matter of Fact from the Second
Jury, that are proper Judges of
it, and should try it; and the*

mat-

ter of *Law from the Learned Judge, that should give the Judgment of Law upon it;* and this is *so plainly proved in the ensuing Discourse,* and hath been *so often in practice, that I know nothing can be said against it.*

Peradventure *some may say,*Sure he that wrote this Book is *Vir Sanguinis,* that desires such severe Justice against every man that kills another man unlawfully, that he must be Indicted of Murther. *Certainly this is a very great mistake, which a considerate Reader, or one that delights not in spilling of Blood, cannot be guilty of; here is no more desired or intended, but that every Person that hath had his Hands in Innocent Blood, receive a full and a legal Trial, according to the Laws of the Land, and the Liberty of a Subject, to be tried at the King's Suit. And I know no Kingdom or Nation in the World, whose Subjects have a fairer, more impartial,*

partial, and indifferent Trial in such Cases, than the Subjects of England *have; who, except (as I have shewed) they become their own Accusers, must be accused by a* Grand Jury, *and convicted or acquitted by another; and afterwards (if guilty) receive Judgment from a Learned and Merciful Judge, according to the Law of the Land.*

I know by the Law of God, amongst the Jews there was a certain Institution, which we call Lex Talionis, An Eye for an Eye, a Tooth for a Tooth, Life for Life; *and that there were Modifications and Qualifications, to abate the extremity of it, in several Cases to be considered, as I have shewed there, is by the Laws of* England *very parallel to them: This is so far from being Sanguinary, that I conceive it would rather prove a Remedy, than a Mischief, rather prevent shedding of Blood, than occasion it; ra-*

ther C

ther *be* Lex Præveniens, *than*
Puniens. *And certainly, who-*
ever opposeth this Opinion, and
proposeth a milder and lighter
way of Trial against one that
hath had his Hands in the Blood
of his Fellow Creature, will hard-
ly himself avoid the Imputati-
on, of a Sanguinary Person.
This way proposed, will prevent
that evil practice (too much u-
sed) of labouring and packing
Grand Jurors, *in point of fa-*
vour, when they are assured be-
fore, that all Accusations, by Grand
Jurors, *for the unlawful kil-*
ling of a Reasonable Creature,
must be Murther. It would con-
duce very much to the dispatch
of the Business in Court., and
be a great ease to Grand Jurors,
that now spend very much un-
necessary time in Questions about
the Law, in such Cases, which
were better spent in examining
the Fact, and leaving the matter
of Law to the Court.

Con-

to the Reader.

Concerning the necessity of this point to be determined, he is a Stranger to the English Laws, and to the English Nation, that over-looks the just and profitable Consequence thereof; there being nothing in this ensuing Tract asserted, but what is agreeable (as I conceive) to the Statute, and Common Laws of this Kingdom, the best allowed Practice, and the Opinions of all the Learned Judges, (at whose Feet I have had the happiness to sit many years, both before the late Civil Wars, and since the happy Restauration of our most Gracious Soveraign) and agreeable to sound Reason, the fullest and best Disquisition after Innocent Blood.

And who can but allow the necessity of it, as to the English Nation at present, when Duels are so frequent in England; it being made matter of Triumph for one Hector

Duellum, quasi duorum bellum.

Done without Authority, is a war against Authority.

(as

The Author

(*as* they call him) to kill another, if it be but for not pledging a Health, or something that looks like an Affront to his Miss, *in placing her at a Ball, in a Playhouse, the Tavern, or the like; and this must not only engage the two differing Parties (although Persons of Quality) to sacrifice their own Lives, and sometimes two. Seconds, or more, Persons of as equal quality, to lose their Lives in the Conflict, or by the Law, (if Death ensue to any of them) in which Contest they are no more concerned, than to second their Friend, and with their own lives to justifie the Quarrel between the two differing Parties, as if both of them had a good Cause, and were in the right, when as sometimes the Occasion is so trivial, not fit for two Boys to dispute.*

That which the Victor thinks to be his honour, proves his dishonour. His Life, his Lands, and Goods, are by Law forfeited, and his Blood corrupted.

Infœlix pugna, ubi majus periculum incumbit victori quam victo.

As

As to what may be Objected to the length of this Tract, I have only this to say, That it is no more than I have accused my self for, and did endeavour to have abstracted and omitted much of it; but when I began to do it, I was overcome by these Considerations, That it was the first Essay of this kind that had been written as a Book; That it was not like to meet with all Readers of like Capacities; some perhaps might gather much out of a little, whereas others would gather but a little out of much, and the whole not of many hours reading, which might be worse spent, and therefore was willing to leave it, as I had first framed it, although I exposed my self to be censured for it.

And because Grand Jurors put so great an Obligation upon the Oath they take as Grand Jurors, and from that (as they conceive) frame so strong an Obje-

ction

ction, _That they are sworn to present all such things and matters as shall be given them in charge; and that the Judges usually, in their charges, dilate and declare the Law, as to all the several Species and Degrees of_ Murther, Manslaughter, _&c. what every unlawful killing of a man is in Law, according to the several Circumstances of the_ Fact: _and therefore they, as_ Grand Jurors, _are bound by their Oath to observe the Circumstances of every_ Fact _before them, what it is in Law as well as in_ Fact, _and so present to the Court both the Law and the_ Fact (Judice inconsulto). _This being the greatest Objection that I have heard from any of them against what is here Asserted; although something is said, as to this Objection, in the ensuing Discourse, I shall here add something more, to clear the point, and answer fully that Objection, by setting down the_

Oath

Oath of a Grand Juror, in terminis, *as also the Oath of a* Juror *of Life and Death, and explain them both:* † You shall diligently inquire, and true presentment make of all such things and matters as shall be given you in charge, or shall come to your knowledge, concerning this present Service. The King's Counsel, your Fellows, and your own, you shall well and truly keep secret. You shall present nothing for malice, or evil will you bear to any person; neither shall you leave any thing unpresented for love, favour, affection, reward, or any hopes thereof; but in all things that shall concern this present Service, you shall present the truth, the whole truth, and nothing else but the truth: So help you God.

In the first place you see by the Oath, they are sworn to be diligent in their Inquiry, not to be sloathful or negligent, being quickned by their Oath: this diligence

† *The Oath of a Grand Juror.*

ligence is to be exercifed in an Inquiry, and this Inquiry is to be made amongft themfelves, in what they know of their own knowledge, or fhall be brought unto them by the Teftimony of others. As to the matter of their Inquiry, which next follows in the Oath, and from which they frame their main Objection, (viz.) all fuch things and matters as fhall be given them in charge: thefe words are general (things and matters) and certainly, in the cleareft Underftanding, are intended the general Heads of all Offences by them Inquirable; As all Murthers, and that comprehends all manner of unlawful killing: All Felonies, and that comprehends all manner of ftealing; and fo of other general Heads of Offences here Inquirable, as Perjuries, Forgeries, Mifdemeanours, &c. although the Learned Judge (where he hath time and leifure) doth in his Charge, when he fpeaks

of

speaks of Murther, declare the several Species and Differences in that Offence by Law; and so of Felony, the several manners of Felonies, simple and compound. And so of other Offences, the words of the Oath so much infisted upon by them do no way oblige them by reason of such a Charge, to determine (by their presentment) every nicety in Law; that may arise upon every Fact before them, otherwise than in that form and matter (according to the nature of the Case) the Court and the King's Council have framed and presented it to their Inquiry, where the single Fact of unlawful killing another, &c. by the hands of such a one, is proved unto them so far, as in their Judgments it is fit matter of Accusation, to bring the whole matter of Fact, and all that may depend upon it, to a farther and more full examination (as is more fully manifested in

B   *the*

the enfuing difcourfe) for fhould
the Judge only give them general
heads of Offences in charge (as
he well may, and many times
doth) without diftinguifhing the
feveral kinds of them, the Grand
Jurors would then want a ground
for this Objection; befides I have
ever taken it, that not only that
which is orally delivered unto
them by the Judge, but that alfo
that is delivered unto them from
the Judge in writing, to be by
them enquired of, is part of their
charge, and that is every Indictment that is prefented unto them,
or other matter in Writing com-
mended by the Court to their Enquiry.

The Juftices in Eyre, that formerly were Itinerant over the
Kingdom (in whofe rooms thefe
Learned Judges fucceed) ever
giving their charge, and whatever was enquirable by the Grand
Jurors in writing; which if fo
underftood (as I know not how it
will be avoided) they are then

by

by their Oath, to present all such things as shall be given them in charge, and so every Indictment of Murther delivered by the Court unto them, is to be found by them, where (as hath been often said) the unlawful killing is so far proved unto them as to make up an Accusation. Then it follows *in the Oath* [The Kings Counsel, their Fellows, and their own they shall keep secret;] *By the* Kings Counsel, *is to be understood any directions the Judge shall in Court give unto them in any matter before them; as also the Evidence of Witnesses, that shall be produced to them on the Kings behalf in any fact (for no other Witnesses must be heard by them) and likewise such Counsellors learned in the Law as shall manage the matter on the Kings behalf (for no other Council is to be heard by them against the Bill) none of this must be revealed or discovered by the* Grand Jurors, *but faithfully kept secret accord-*

B 2   *ing*

ing to their *Oath from the party concerned, his friends, and all others, except the Court demand any question from them upon their Evidence;* so likewise must they keep their Fellow Jurors Counsel, and their own, *that is, they are not to discover what any one of themselves have together counselled, advised, or debated, in the business before them against such a person. They are the Kings great Council upon this account, and all such great Councils where the King is so much concerned, take an Oath of Secrecy, for otherwise by revealing such Counsels, a Traytor, a Murtherer, and the greatest Felon may escape, to the endangering of King and Kingdom; and this offence in ancient time was holden for Treason or Felony.*

Stamf. fol. 36.
27. lib. Aff.

In George's *Case in* Anno 27. lib. Aff. *upon his Indictment was acquitted; but the* Lo. Coke *in his* third Institutes fol. 107. *says,* Certain it is, that such discovery is accompanied with Perjury, and a

great

great Misprision to be punished by Fine and Imprisonment. *And it is well provided by the Oath, that each Juror is sworn to keep his own Counsel also; for he that will not keep his own secrets, will hardly keep anothers.*

So much for the matter of the Oath, what they are to do; It *follows in the Oath, with what Integrity they ought to do their duty,* They are to present no person for any offence, through any malice they have to the person, nor omit any meerly for any favour they have for the per-son: *This is so plain, it needs nothing but practice; these two seem very easie, but indeed are very difficult to flesh and blood, Not to take revenge when one hath power to do it, and not to shew favour when there is power and opportunity to express it; not but that a Grand Juror may present another he is at difference withal, if there be a real and true cause for it, but it must not*

be

be done from malice, and by way
of revenge, in presenting such a
person, before another as guilty.
Malice and Favour (two great
enemies to Justice) are to be excluded all Courts of Justice, as
too partial; and therefore the
Oath well concludes, That they
shall present the truth, the whole
truth, and nothing but the truth:
all these three expressions of truth
have relation to the fact of Murther, or unlawful killing (for I
shall in this place apply it to that
Offence) in a legal sense, as to
legal proceedings; The truth,
that is, Truth sufficient to make
an accusation against a nocent person; The whole truth, not con-
cealing any part of it wilfully,
but so presenting it, that the whole
matter of fact concerning the unlawful killing another may come
in question to another Jury, which
cannot be unleß it be found Murther; the Common Law account-
ing all felonious and unlawful
killing a reasonable Creature Mur-

ther

ther, *until the difference and di-*
stinction appear upon the Verdict
of another Jury, that are to try it,
and the Judgment of the Court in
point of Law upon that Verdict.
Observe the Note in the
Margent, what that Sta-
tute says ; adjudicetur
coram Justiciar. *It shall*
be adjudged by the Judg-
es or Justices (not the
Grand Jury) what is
Manslaughter per Infor-
tunium; *and it can never*
be adjudged by the Judges, but
when it is tried before them,
which cannot be upon an Indict-
ment of per Infortunium *only (as*
is more fully observed in the fol-
lowing discourse ;) Observe like-
wise what follows in that Sta-
tute, Sed locum habeat Murdrum
de interfectis per feloniam. *So*
that by this Statute, *all felonious*
killing is Murther still, as it was
at the Common Law before, and
that Statute *is not to be repealed by*
Grand Jurors.

Murdrum de cætero non adjudicetur coram Justiciar. ubi infortunium tantummodo adjudicatum est,sed locum habeatMurdrum de interfectis per feloniam tantum , & non aliter. *Statut. de Marlebridge* 52 H.3.c.26.

B 4   And

The Author

And as there must not be in the Grand Jury, Suppreſſio veri, *a ſuppreſſion or leſſening of the truth; ſo there must not be* Expreſſio falſi, *a falſe Accuſation; both are to be avoided, and therefore it follows in the* Oath, And nothing but the truth, *that is, no known falſity, no falſe Accuſation againſt any perſon* must *be preſented, whereby to bring an Innocent perſon to trial, where there is nothing of the fact to be proved againſt him, or any probable Accuſation; if theſe three* Truths, *in this Oath mentioned, are not to be underſtood in this legal ſenſe, and according to the common practice of legal proceedings in theſe caſes; I must confeſs I am to be inſtructed how any* Grand Juror (*that hears but one ſide) can ſatiſfie his* * Conſcience, *that in a plain literal and* Grammatical *ſenſe, he can ſwear that* every Preſentment and Indictment *that comes from the* Grand Jury with

* Utramque partem, in-audias, ne judices. Qui judicat aliquid (parte inaudita altera) licet æquum judicaret haud æquus eſt. Yet Grand Jurors take themſelves to be Judges of the Fact.

with a Billa vera , *contains in it,* the truth, the whole truth, and nothing but the truth ; *and this is cleared by the laft words of the* Oath, [According to their beft skill and knowledge] *for this muft be underftood, skill and knowledge in the Law and Fact , as to the practice and nature of the proceedings of the Law in fuch cafes ; for it is rather* difcretio legis *than* hominis,

And thus have I, according to my beft fenfe and underftanding of the Oath, *explained it, and anfwered the common Objection to it , by making it appear , that there is nothing in the Oath that any way obligeth them againft what I have either here , or in the enfuing difcourfe ; advifed them unto. And that this may yet be more evident (becaufe I would make it as plain as I can, though with too many Tautologies and Repetitions) I fhall alfo in* terminis *fet down the Oath of the* Jurors of *Life and Death,*
by

this is not in the form of the Oath before mentioned.

by which it doth appear, that they only stand charged with the Prisoner (as it is exprest in the Oath) and the Grand Jury only with the Accusation against him;

Potty Jurys Oath

[You shall well and truly try, and true deliverance make between our Sovereign Lord the King and the Prisoner at the Bar (whom you shall have in Charge) and a true Verdict give according to your Evidence; So help you God.] *Which is to be formally and legally drawn up in the nature of a Declaration at Law at the Kings suit, the King being Plaintiff and the Prisoner Defendant, which the Prisoner upon his Arraignment either confesseth, and then he is convicted without hearing of any Evidence against him, or otherwise pleads* Not guilty *to it, to which the* King (by the Clerk of the Crown) joyns Issue by Cul prit, *viz.* that he is ready to prove him guilty; *and so the Issue being thus joyned, Evidence for the King is given*

against

againſt him upon Oath, to which he makes his defence in perſon, or by * *Council (if any point of Law a-riſe to which he deſires Council, and the Court approve of it, the Judge being as well of Council for the Priſoner as the King) calls his Witneſſes (if he have any) who ſpeak upon their Credits, and not upon their Oaths, which is much for the advantage of the Priſoner, the Law preſuming (in favour of life) the Affirmative proof to be ſo clear againſt the Pri-ſoner, that nothing in the* † *Negative can be pro-ved (upon Oath) againſt it; and after a full trial of what can be ſaid and proved on both ſides, and a convenient time taken by the Jury to conſider of it, they bring in their Verdict, either convict him or acquit him; either find him guilty according to the Indictment found*

* If he have Council, he muſt pray it before he plead *Not guilty*, he cannot after. 3. *Inſt. fol.* 129.

† And that is one reaſon why regularly he cannot have Council. The ſecond reaſon is, the Court ought to ſee the Indictment, Trial, and other proceedings good in Law, leſt by an erroneous Judgment they attaint the Priſoner. 3. *Inſt.* 137. *fol.* 29.

found by the Grand Jury *by hear-ing of one side, or specially as they find the fact by hearing of both sides; for they are not bound strictly to the matter and form of the* Indictment, *as the* Grand Jury *have found it, for they may by Law extenuate it to the least degree of offence, that can be in that kind, but they cannot aggravate it, or exceed above what the* Grand Jury *have found; for if they might do so, they would become Accusers as well as Tryers, which would be against the Laws and liberty of the Subject: And therefore the* Grand Jurors *have the greater reason, to enlarge in their Declaration or Accusation for the King (as in all Declarations at Law is usual) as far as the Law will heighten all offences in Blood, since the other Jury have so much liberty to lessen the damages, and extenuate the Crime, whatever the Accusation is.*
Now

Secta pacis *is by* Indictment, *which is the* King's Suit, *and as it were his* Declaration. *The* King *formerly did not pardon* homicidium, *but* Sectam pacis nostræ quæ ad nos pertinet de homicidiis. 3. Inst. fol. 235.

*Now upon what I have writ-
ten in this Preface, and the
Book, I am not ignorant how
much I have subjected my self*
ad captum Lectoris, *to the vari-
ous censures of the several Readers, especially such as use to
serve, or may serve on Grand
Juries, Gentlemen I know of
the best quality next to the Peers
of the Realm, and in which Em-
ployment for their King and Country it is an honour to serve; And
I hope it will be no dishonour nor
indignity to any of them to enter-
tain, or at least to peruse this Advice, how they may with the
greatest prudence and fidelity pass
through an Enquiry after Iino-
cent Bloodshed; when they are
called unto it, and leave nothing
therein (of this Crying Sin) to be
repented of, that it was not fully
Enquired of by them, that so
their exact care and Justice may
keep themselvas secure from the
guilt of Innocent blood.*

I

I doubt not but it will meet with some Readers so possessed with the contrary Opinion, by an erroneous practice or misunderstanding of the Laws, and of the Grand Jurors Oath, that so soon as they read the Title will cast away the Book and cry, a Paradox; Others happily more unbiassed in their Opinions, and of more moderation and ingenuity (if they dislike) will publickly confute it, with stronger arguments and grounds of Law and Reason, and better experience in point of practice, and so determine the point; and in that I shall have my end.

I am very certain, that I entred not upon this Subject with an offensive mind, but cum moderamine inculpatæ tutelæ, not with a direct design to kill any, but rather to fright, weaken, and drive away that Dæmon of Passion in man to commit Murther, and to give the best advice to Grand Jurors in Cases of Blood.

A

to the Reader.

A small thing, oft times, hath the power to redreß a great Inconvenience, yea, to take up a cruel Feud; as Virgil *faith, of that of* Bees *when they are actually engaged in battel,*

Hi motus animorum atque hæc
certamina tanta,

Pulveris exigui jactu compreffa
quiefcent.

ADVICE

ADVICE

TO

Grand JURORS

IN

Cases of Blood.

T is the great happiness, freedom, and liberty of the *English*
Nation, that (in all
common and ordinary
Trials) of offences Criminal and
Capital, as Treasons, Murthers,
Felonies and Misdemeanors, each
Freeman (and so are all the people

of *England*, as to this) fhall receive his Trial *per pares*, by his equals ; which is well provided for by the great Charter of the Liberties of *England*, in thefe words ; *No Free-man fhall be taken, or Imprifoned, or diffeifed of his Freehold, Liber-ties, or Free-cuftomes, nor be Out-lawed, banifhed, or in any manner deftroyed,&c. but by lawful Judg-ment of his Peers, or by the Law of the Land.* This Chapter of *Magna Charta* is partly repeated in a later Statute, (*a*) and there *Law of the Land* is expounded [*Indict-ment*] procefs by Writ original, and courfe of the Law : Another Sta-tute recites it, and inftead of the words *Law of the Land*, puts in Procefs of the Law, as *equivalent* and *Synonimous*, fignifying the fame thing. And again, a Statute of that King fays, (*b*) *No man fhall anfwer without Prefentment be-fore the Juftices, or matter of Re-cord, or by due Procefs and Writ original*, according to the old Law of the Land, (*c*) as it is well ob-ferved

(a) 25 E. 3. 4.
5 E. 3. 9.
42 E. 3. 3.
Vit. Abbot St.
Alban. 143.

(b) 37 E. 3. 18.

(c) Cook 3.
Inft. Tit. Indict.
136.

ferved by the Lo. *Cook* (that Oracle of the Law) *In pleas of the Crown, and other Common offences and Nufances, the King cannot (in an ordinary way) put any man to anfwer; but he muft be apprifed by Indictment, or other matter of Record.* For, by the Law of the Land, a Felon or a Murtherer cannot be convicted (d) or attainted (though he confefs the Felony or Murther) until a grand Jury have prefented the offence; nor can any perfon (generally and ordinarily be convicted or attainted, or have Judgment of life, or Member)upon any Criminal accufation; but there muft be two Juries pafs upon him, at leaft 24 perfons, the one a Grand Jury (*ex parte Regis*) to prefent the offence fit for a trial; the other a petit or leffer Jury, *inter Regem, & perfonam accufat.* to try the truth of that Prefentment (e). The Grand Jury coming from all parts of the Coun-

by Verdict; but the Offence muft be found by twenty four.

(d) *Except by utlawry.*

(e) *No Peer, or Subject, can be Convicted*

C 2   ty,

ty (*f*), the other Jury of the very neighbourhood *de vici-netto*, where the offence was committed; for, *vicini vicinorum facta optime præsumuntur scire*; and so in probability of Law, are presumed to know something experimentally (besides what they have by Testimony) both of the quality of the person, truth, and nature of the offence, with all its circumstances, and happily the credit of the Accuser and his Witnesses. It is not sufficient that they dwell in the County, but they are to be of the Neighbourhood, nay, *le plus procheins* to the place of the fact, as by *Artic. super cap.* 9. it is appointed; They must be most near, most sufficient, and least suspicious, *ibid.* The first being called a *Grand Jury*, or a Great Jury, either in respect of their number, being above twelve, (the general certainty of all other Juries) and may be as many as the

(*f*) *It is not sufficient, that they dwell in the County, but they are to be of the Neighbourhood; nay,* le plus procheines *to the place of the fact;* as *by* Artic. super cap. 9. *it is appointed,* They must be most near, most sufficient, and least suspicious. ibid.

the Court pleafe, but ufually exceed not 23, and in good prudence
(when there is much, or weighty
bufinefs) there ought not to be a
leffer number, for if there be lefs
or more, they may be fo divided,
that there can be no verdict (as by
experience hath been obferved)
for lefs than twelve agreeing, cannot make a Legal verdict: Or
they are called *Grand* in refpect
of the quality of their Perfons,
and greatnefs of their Eftates, a-
bility of their Judgments (being
of good Education) or laftly
(which I conceive the beft reafon)
that, *propter excellentiam*, they
are ftyled (g) *Juratores pro Do-*
mino Rege pro Corpore Com. Jurors for our Soveraign Lord the
King for the County of *S.* and as
the Commons in Parliament are
to the whole Kingdom, they have
an unlimited power to prefent all
offences committed in their County, that are *contra Pacem, Coro-*
nam, & dignitatem Regis, againft
the Peace, the Crown, and dignity

(g) *The King's*
Jury.

C 3   of

of the King, againſt either Statute or Common Law, they being the great and grand Spring, or *Primum mobile* of the Court, that gives motion to all the other wheels; their Preſentment being the key, that either opens or ſhuts the proceedings of the Court in every offence. And therefore it is that the Law of *England* takes care, that as well the Grand Jury, as the other Jury, conſiſt of perſons that are *probi*, & *legales homines*, good and lawful men; each man muſt be *probus*, *quaſi probatus*, an approved honeſt man; *vel a Græc.* Πρεσάγεν, & *qui progredi poſſit prægredi debet*, he that will go on in vertue, certainly ought principally to be choſen to attend the Courts of Juſtice. It is called, *Juſtitia, quaſi juris ſtatio, vel ſtatus, quod per Juſtitiam, jus ſtat,* i. *exercetur.* (*h*) It is called *Juſtice* becauſe it is the Standard of Right, *miſera ſervitus ubi Jus vagum.* *Juſtice* being one of the Cardinal vertues ought to be attended

(h) *Jus à Jovis nomine. Jus qu.* Jovis os; *omne enim Jus & Juſtitia à Deo eſt.*

attended by none but the *virtuoso,*
the moſt vertuous, pious, and in-
genuous perſons; *probi* ſignifying,
not only *faithful,* but *skilful;*
none can be preſumed to be faithful in keeping an Oath,
(*i*) that wants skill to
know how to perform his
duty; What expectation
can there be of a good
Verdict, from a bad or
ignorant man? Can he
that is not capable to un-
derſtand a Cauſe, ever
make a right Judgment
of it? Will a Liar preſent
a truth; a Thief convict
his fellow thief; a Man of
blood a Murtherer? or,
Who can expect Juſtice from him
who neither to his God nor to
himſelf is juſt, or true? He that
believes Judges are *quaſi Dei, Gods*
(as the Scripture calls them) or
that God ſits amongſt, and is preſent with Judges in Judgment (as
in the Scripture ſenſe it is truth,
and ought to be believed) cannot

(1) v. Statut.3 Ed.1.c.11. Foraſmuch *as many being* indicted *of Murther, and* culpable *of the ſame, by fa-*vourable *Inqueſts taken by* the Sheriff, *and by the Kings* Writ *of* Odio & Atia *be* replevied *unto the coming of the Juſtices in Eyre. It is provided ſuch Inqueſts ſhall be taken by lawful men choſen out by Oath (of whom two at the leaſt ſhall be Knights) which, by no affinity with the priſoner, or otherwiſe, are to be ſuſ-pected.*

5 H.7. fol. 5.
Coke l.9. f.56.
9 H.3. c.25.
6 Ed.1. c.9.
Regiſt.fol.133.

but

but apprehend how unreasonable
it is, to bring such a Jury before
such a presence, to act in a con-
cernment of so high a nature, as
the life of a Man; *whose* verdict
ought to be *veredictum*, a true

Juramentum quod mente Juratur.

saying, *quoddam Evangelium*, as
the Gospel they swear upon, *dictum
veritatis*, the saying of Truth it
self (especially as it is the verdict
of the Jury of life and death) who
have the advantage of hearing, not
only the Accuser and his Witnesses, but also the party accused, and
his Witnesses face to face. They

(k) In respect of the Grand Jury.

are called, although a (*k*) Petty
Jury, yet a Jury of life and death,
which the Grand Jury are not;
although they enquire of the same
offence, from the great power in
their hands to acquit or condemn
the life of a man, according to
their evidence. Upon whose verdict, the Judge according to Law
grounds the Judgment of life or
death, of acquittal or condemnation; and as a Jury may give a
just verdict (as to themselves)
upon

upon a falſe Teſtimony given to
them, ſo may the Judge (as to
himſelf) give. a juſt Judgment
upon a falſe verdict given by the
Jury. For as the Jurors are excuſable, that give their verdict, *ſe-*
cundum allegata, *& probata*, *per*
ſacrum Teſtimonium, by what is
alledged and proved to them by
the Oaths of Witneſſes, or confeſſion of the party; even ſo that
Judge is excuſable (*in foro Con-*
ſcientiæ) that gives Judgment upon a verdict (though falſe) for he
doth not therein *Jus dare*, but *Jus*
dicere ſecundum verediĉt. Jur.
upon the verdict of the Petit Jury
and preſentment of a Grand Jury,
and this is fully verified in two remarkable (*l*) Cafes noted
in the Margent; a ſufficient caution to all Judges,
not to try any for Mur-
ther, where they have
not an infallible evidence
of the death of the party ſlain.

And as every Juror ought to be
probus homo, an honeſt and a skilful

(l) Coke *Inſtit.*3.*fol.*232.
Glouc. *Aſſizes xiij.*Car.2.
Regis (Harriſon's *caſe*)
Nimia præcipitatio & mo-
roſa cunctatio; two dan-
gerous extreams.

ful man, fo ought every one to be *legalis homo*, a perfon fo qualified that the Law allows of; for a man may be an honeft, prudent, and juft man, and yet in the eye of the Law not a lawful Jury-man; for in one fenfe he is not *legalis homo*, that is not *ligeus & fubditus Dom.*

*vi.*Coke 3.*Inft.* *fo.*32.*tit.* Petit Treafon.

Regis Angliæ, for the Law provides that the Kings Liege people fhall be tried *per pares*, by their equals, their fellow Subjects: In a proper fenfe he is faid, in Law, not to be *legalis homo*, that is *homo utlagatus*, an outlawed perfon, one that is *extra legem pofitus*; who is no better than one that is *extraneus*, an alien, a ftranger, one not only put out of the protection of the Law, but fuch a one as the Law will have nothing to do with (as he fo ftands) in Courts of Juftice, to ferve as a Juror; nay, fuch a perfon being a Juror, will make the verdict void, and it is a good exception in arreft of Judgment, that any of the Jurors were outlawed. But in a larger fenfe he *is*

not

not *legalis homo*, such a legal and indifferent person (as the Law requires) who is either in such a degree of blood to the prisoner, as the Law presumes him partial, or in such an evil reputation, as the Law presumes him unjust; for as it is not fit for a Father to be of a Jury to try his Son, or the Son the Father; Brothers, Uncles, or near Relations to try one another, so it is not fit that he that is *particeps criminis*, or indeed *criminalis homo*, a man that stands judicially accused, indicted, convicted, or attainted for Felony, to try another for Felony (or indeed to be a grand Juror to present it) the Law provides that each Juror ought to be a person, *rectus in Curia*, that stands right in Court, above and against all natural, rational, and legal exceptions. *Qui accusat integræ famæ sit & non criminosus*; for certainly, to clear the matter of fact (as a Juror of life and death) and wisely to discern the Cause in question,

He *is* liber & legalis homo, *that is a man of fame and credit, that doth enjoy* liberam legem. Coke 3.*Inst.fol.*22. 11 H.4. Coke 3.*Inst. fol.*32.

upon

upon a doubtful and perplext Evidence, many times, requires as
great ability in the Jurors of life
and death, as in the Judge to examine the caufe, and to give Judgment upon the Verdict; there being much more of Black-art ufed
to darken and obfcure the truth of
the fact (in cafes of Bloud) a-
mongft the Jurors (efpecially if
either a great Perfon, or rich, be
concerned therein) than poffibly
can be, to prevent or prevaricate a
right Judgment, in the Judge; or
by any duft of gold, power or favour, to put out his eyes, or falfifie
his clear fight, who fits every way
above fuch a temptation.

The Jurors of *England* (efpecially in the Circuits) with their
unequal yoke-fellows the *Tales-
men*, are (for the moft part) the
very fcandal of the Laws practical
of *England*, who feldom ferve, but
to ferve a turn (*m*), to obey a Su-
periour, pleafure a Friend, or to

(*m*) 'Tis hard to
get an unbiaffed
Jury. Some ferv-
ing, that had
more need to be relieved by the & d. than difcretion to fift out the
truth of the fact.

help

help away (in a hurry) a quick difpatch of practice: This fault is not in the Laws of *England*, but the male execution of them. The Statute of the 27 *Eliz. c. 6.* provides that each Juror fhould have at leaft four pounds *per annum* in Lands, Tenements, or Rents; and this muft be their fufficiency, where the (*n*) debt or damages (or both together) amount to forty marks. The general courfe of the world being to efteem men according to their Eftates, *Quantum quif-que fua nummorum fervat in arca, tantum habet & fidei.* Jurors that have Eftates to lofe, will be afraid to commit perjury. The beft things abufed, alwaies prove the worft; the fweeteft Wine makes the fharpeft Vinegar, not that the fault is in the Wine, but in the ufe and abufe of it: were better care taken in return of Jurors (*o*), I dare fay, the trial by *twelve*

(*n*) Coke 1. *Inft.*272.

(*o*) In ancient time the Jury, as well in Common Pleas as in Pleas of the Crown, were twelve Knights. Glanvile *lib.* 2. *c.* 14. & Bract.*fol.*116.

would

would not be more ancient than excellent; the Excellency of it appears, in the long, conſtant, and general uſe of it amongſt the people of *England*. This way of trial, to have all their Eſtates, Injuries, and Lives tried by twelve men, and thoſe Neighbours, of our own degree and parity, and without exception (upon a lawful challenge) certainly nothing can be ſaid more for the commendation of it, than the conſtant practice, and unanimous approbation of it in *England*, to this day, ſince the firſt beginning of it: The trial by *twelve* being very ancient, though Mr. *Daniel*, and *Polydor Virgil* deny it to be ancienter than the *Norman* Conqueſt. *But Polydor* (as ſays the excellent Sr. *H. Savil*) *was an* Italian, *and a ſtranger in our Common-wealth, and ſo deceived!* (*p*) It is of *Engliſh Saxon* deſcent, as by the Laws of King *Etheldred*, *cap.* 4. thus; *In all Hundreds let Aſſemblies be, and twelve Free-men of the*

(*p*) Lamb. *in verbo Centur.* D. Spelman *in Jurat. vide Conſult. de Martic.* Walliæ *v.*3.

in Cases of Blood.   15

*the most ancient together shall
swear, not to condemn the Innocent, nor absolve the guilty.* It
was in use with the *French*, in the
Age of *Charlemaine*. They that
would see more of this, let them
read that learned and ancient Book
written by Judge *Fortescue*, in
commendation of the Laws of
England. I shall leave this Subject, having briefly touched upon
the happiness and liberty the Subjects of *England* enjoy, to have
their trials for their Estates and
Lives, *per pares*, by Juries of
twelve men ; what manner of
persons Grand Jurors and those
Jurors ought to be, and of the
excellency and antiquity of such
trials ; in the next place (after I
have shewed the heynousness of
Murther, both by the Laws of
God, and the Laws of this Land, and
made some little parallel therein)
I shall briefly shew, That it is
the duty of all Grand Jurors, in all
Cases of blood, touching the death
of any reasonable creature, by
violence,

violence, or by the hand or act of any other reasonable Creature, where the Bill of Indictment is brought unto them for Murther, in case they find, upon the Evidence, any probability that the person said to be killed in the Indictment, was slain by the person charged to do it in the Indictment) to put *Billa vera* to that Indictment, without foreclosing the Court, by judging amongst themselves the points of Law that may arise in that case, as whether it be Murther, Manslaughter, at Common Law, or upon the Statute *Se def. per Infortunium*, Justifiable, or otherwise; none of these special matters being to be found by them that are but Inquisitors and Accusers for the King; not tryers of the offence, hearing but Witnesses on one side, and whose presentment, or verdict, is not final, but must be put to Issue betwixt the King and the party to be tried by another Jury, whether there be truth in it or no, whatever the

practice

practice of Grand Jurors hath been (of late) to the contrary; this being the chief aim and defign of this Tract.

I have not met with any amongſt Chriſtians, and I believe there is none amongſt Heathens, or rational Creatures, but believe, whatever their practices are to the contrary, that the ſhedding of Innocent bloud is a great offence, a crying ſin.   To take away the life of a Plant, is but the vigour in the juyce; and the life of a Beaſt, is but the vigour in the bloud; but the life of a Man is a (r) *ſpirit*, and ſpiritual ſubſtance, the breath of God breathed into him, and not to be extinguiſhed unjuſtly by the hand of man.   Certainly, *vox ſanguinis eſt vox clamantis*, it is one of the four ſins (s) that the Scripture calls, *Clamantia Peccata*, Crying Sins, that cry to God for vengeance (even in this world) upon the Manſlayer.   Immediately after the Floud God

(r) Gen. 9. 4.

(s) *Sunt vox clamorum, vox ſanguinis &* Sodomorum, *vox oppreſſorum, mercis detenta laborum.*

D   com-

commanded, that blood unjuftly
fhed fhould be required by the
Magiftrate of the Manquiller. It
is within the *Magna Charta* of
God himfelf, and by an Act of
Parliament made in Heaven, never
to be repealed, It is enacted, that
he that fheds mans blood, by man
fhall his blood be fhed. At the hand
of every mans Brother will I re-
quire the life of man, fays God
himfelf (*t*). God many times allowed of *Reftitution*, and other
fatisfactions in other Felonies, but
never in cafe of blood; for, *who*
can make fatisfaction for the life of
a Man ?

(t) *Solus Deus*
qui vitam
dat vitæ eft
Dominus ; nec
poteft quifquam
eam jufte aufer-
re nifi Deus,
vel gerens au-
thoritatem Dei,
ut Judex.

And this was the reafon, that amongft Chriftians it was not lawful for the Lord to kill his Villain.

The firft Murtherer that we
read of was the Devil, who the
Scripture fays, *was a Murtherer*
from the beginning ; in quantum
*traxit in peccatum,*in drawing our
Firft Parents into fin, and fo to
death. The next that we read of
(for

(for the Devil would not be long before he had tempted more to his own fin) was *Cain*, that kill'd his Brother *Abel*, and it feems very defperately fhed much of his blood in many parts of his body, for the word is in the Plural number, *vox Sanguinum*, the voice of his *Bloods*; or, becaufe the Bloods of the future pofterity of *Abel* (that he might have had) were fhed in him, by the Murther of *Cain*. It is true that *Cain's* blood was not fhed by that Law, although he kill'd his Brother, the World being not then peopled, nor that Law then fo pofitively given by God, and the example and terrour to others could not then be fo great (which is oft the great end of punifhment, *ut pœna ad paucos metus ad omnes perveniat*;) and therefore *Cain* was to furvive by God's fpecial appointment, not by any favour of God towards him, but that he might have Gods mark (as a Murtherer) upon him, to the Terrour of all

D 2   others

others that fhould fee him. What vifible mark and diftinction this was, is but conjectured at ; fome think it was a horrible fhaking over his whole body, as the *Septuagint* tranflate , who , for *Thou fhalt be a Vagabond and Runagate*,

read, *He fhould* (*n*) *figh and tremble* ; or an exceeding fhame and confufion, in that he ran from place to place to hide himfelf; or fome vifible mark in his face , as *Lyranus* thinketh : Some *Hebrews* think it was a horn in his forehead ; fome, a letter ; fome , that a Dog led him. The Scripture is plain, that for this Murther he was to be a *Fugitive, and a Vagabond upon the face of the Earth* ; one (as the Text fays) that *went from the prefence of the Lord* , to whom the Earth was accurfed ; and certainly the guilt and fhame he carried about him , like the bloody *Jews* that murthered Chrift, and are to this day Vagabonds over the Earth ; or thofe bloody furviving Regicides , that mur-

murthered the beft of Kings (*x*) *(x) K. Charles the Firft.*
(yet live, with that black mark of
King-killing upon them) was, and
is, a Judgment greater than death
it felf; as it is in the *Pfalms* (*y*), *(y) Pfal.59.11.*
Slay them not left my people for-
get it: but fcatter them abroad
amongft the people, and put them
down, O Lord, our defence. And
that was the Judgment of *Cain*,
who before his natural death
(fome fay) was kill'd by *Lamech*,
who fhot in a Bufh at a Beaft, and
kill'd *Cain* (*z*). And the *Turks* *(z) Theod. quæft. 44. in Gen.*
at this day believe, that at the
Day of Judgment, when the
Grave and Hell fhall deliver up
their dead, *Cain*, that Fratricide
and murtherer, fhall lead, and be
as it were the Captain of the
damned in Hell.

Amongft all the Laws of God,
which he himfelf appointed the
Ifraelites (his own People) when
they were to inhabite *Canaan*, the
Land of Promife, there was not
any mercy, or City of Refuge
appointed for a Murtherer or Man-
           D 3   .   flayer,

flayer, but only where it was done unawares; as feveral clear Cafes are put in Scripture to make this plain, 35 *Numb.23.v. If one throw a Stone that a man die thereof (and faw him not) but did it unawares.* So the 19.*Deut.5. When a man goeth to the wood with his Neighbour* (mark how ftrongly this Cafe is put, with his Neighbour, his Friend, whom he had no unkindnefs for) *to hew wood, and as his hand fetcheth a ftroak with the Axe to cut down the Tree, the head flippeth of from the helve and fmiteth his Neighbour that he die* ; in thefe, and many fuch like cafes there put, *he fhall flee to the City of Refuge, and ftay there until the Congregation fhall judge betwixt the Manflayer, and the Avenger of blood, whether he did it wittingly, or unawares.* The *Hebrews* underftand by the *Congregation*, the *Senators* and *Chief Judges* of the City; and although it were done *unawares*, and fo adjudged by the Congregation, yet

35.Numb.23.

29.Deut.5.

yet fo hainous was the offence of
Blood before God (though nothing of mans will. in it) that
even fuch Manflayer was never
(during his life) afterwards to de-
part from the City until it was fo
adjudged by the Congregation, or
until the death of the High-Prieft,
(who was a type of Chrift that
fet us all free ;) for if he did de-
part, then the Avenger of blood,
(who was next Kinfman to the
party flain) might, if he met him,
juftifie the killing of him. So it is
very apparent, that before thefe
Cities of Refuge were appointed
for mercy to him that had killed
another unawares, fuch a Manflayer might have been killed by
the Avenger of blood, as well as
he that had killed another wilfully : and after they were ordained, they could not be intended to fhew Mercy, or to be an
Afylum or Sanctuary for any that
had willingly, wilfully, or by a
paffionate affault killed another.
If it be objected (as what fin or
D 4   offender

offender is there that hath not his Advocate) that it is faid in the 19. of *Deut.* 11.v . *But if any man hate his Neighbour, and lay await for him, and rife againft him and fmite him that he die, and then flie to any of thofe Cities, he fhall be fetcht thence, and delivered into the hands of the Avenger of blood, that he may die. Thine eye* (though the tendereft part thou haft) *fhall not fpare him* (how comely foever his perfon may feem) *but thou fhalt put Innocent blood from* Ifrael, *that it may go well with thee* (*a*).   If it fhall be inferr'd from hence, That the Cities of Refuge were ordained for all forts of Manflaughter, but where it was done of malice, forethought, ancient hatred, or with a fedate and malicious mind; hereby implying, that he that kills another upon a fudden quarrel, affault, or in heat of blood (as it is termed) might flie to a City of Refuge, and find Sanctuary ; It muft needs be upon a very great miftake.

19. Deut. 11.

(a) i.e. with the Magiftrate and People.

miftake. Nor can the Judicials of
God herein (put into feveral plain
and illuftrating Cafes by God himfelf) be reconciled if it fhould be
fo underftood : It is faid in the
31. *Exod.* 13. *If a man lay not
wait , but God deliver him into
his hands, then I will appoint
thee a place whither he shall flie.*
The meaning of the *delivering
him into his hands*, muft of neceffity be underftood of fuch a
providence that could not be fore-
feen, and fo not poffible to be prevented by the Manflayer, where-
in there could be nothing of his
will , but purely chance and unawares , as in the Cafes put before
of cafting the Stone , and killing
one he faw not ; cutting of the
wood, and falling of the helm of
the Axe, or Bough from the Tree ;
where many fuch Examples might
be given, which the Law of *England* now fums up in one head or
Reafon, *viz.* (*b*) Where one is (*b*) *utrum quis
dederit operam
rei licitæ an illicitæ.* Stamf.lib.1. fol. 12.

doing

doing a lawful and juſtifiable act in his Trade, Calling, or lawful Recreation, and by chance and unawares, another happens to be kill'd by him, then he ſhall have a Pardon of courſe now inſtead of a City of Refuge (as ſhall be hereafter ſhewed) for it is very plain by expreſs places of Scripture, that all other voluntary killing of a man unlawfully, found no Mercy, no City of Refuge, but there the Manſlayer was to die by the hand of the Avenger of blood (it appearing ſo before the Magiſtrate or Congregation :) As to inſtance in ſome few Caſes out of Scripture. 21.*Exod.*12. *He that ſmiteth a man that he die, ſhall be ſlain for it :* if any deſtruction follow, there he ſhall give life for life (except it be unawares.) So in the 16, 17, 18. v. of the 31. of *Numbers, If any man ſmite another with an inſtrument of Iron that he die, then he is a murtherer, and the Murtherer ſhall die for it. If he ſmite him by throwing a Stone that*

21.Exod.12.

31.Numb.16, 17,18.

that he die, he that fmote him is a Murtherer, let the fame murther-er be flain; therefore the Avenger of blood himfelf fhall flay the Murtherer. When he meeteth him he *fhall flay him* (mark the Ingemination,) *he fhall furely flay him,* as it is in the 21. *Exod.* 12. He *that fmiteth a man that he die, fhall die the death;* that is, *fhall furely die;* for this doubling of the word, *importat majorem certitudinem,* importeth greater certainty; and yet in all thefe Cafes, not one word of *malice, lying in wait,* or *enmity.* (c) It is a general Law, He that killeth fhould be killed again, and this Law is grounded upon the Law of Nature; for like as it is agreeable to Nature, *ut putridum membrum abfcindatur, ut reliqua confervatur,* that a rotten member fhould be cut off that the reft may be preferved; fo a Murtherer is to be killed, *ne plures occidantur,* left more fhould be killed. This Law

All thefe fuddain Actions.

(c) *He that fmiteth another that he die;* five intendat occidere, five non, *fhall die.*

Law is given unto *Noah* , *Gen.* 9. when the World was reſtored ; and here it is but repeated and renewed. The Laws of other Nations herein conſent with *Mo-ſes :* The *Athenians* did ſeverely puniſh Murther , expelling the Murtherer from the Temple of the Gods, and from all Society and Colloquy of Men, till he had his Judgment. And by the Law *Cornelia,* among the *Romans* , He which had killed another with ſword , or poyſon, or by falſe Teſtimony, loſt his head, if he were of the better ſort ; if of meaner condition , he was hanged on the Croſs , or caſt unto Wild beaſts, that was himſelf like a Tiger a-mongſt men ; *Simler.* And the reaſon of the ſeverity was, becauſe Murtherers deface the Image of God in Man *(d)*, and lay violent hands to take away his temporal

(d) By *Murther* a *reaſonable Creature is loſt,* which all the World cannot *reſtore.* Trees, though they be cut down grow again, but a *Man once ſlain can never be recovered.* Pericl. apud Plut. in ipſius vita. And for the moſt part , unleſs the Mercy of God be the greater, the Soul is loſt with the Body.

life,

life, for whom Chrift died to give eternal life. A King (an inferiour god) would take it ill to have his Image, his Picture, wilfully ftab'd through and cut in pieces by any, becaufe it is his. It is very plain, by the Judicials of God, that where there was any wilful fmiting, or ftriking (though fuddenly, and from a prefent paffion, occafioned by a fudden provocation) whereby death followed, in which the will, fury (which is a temporary madnefs) affent, or affault of the Manflayer, might appear, there was no City of Refuge, or Mercy, by Gods Law provided for it; only what was done unawares, and unforefeen (as aforefaid) found a City of Refuge, otherwife what can be meant by thofe words, *unawares*, and where *he faw him not*: and in thefe very Cafes of killing another, *ex improvifo*, unawares, or by misfortune, for whom there was a City of Refuge provided (by God himfelf) yet there the
Avenger

Avenger of blood, if he overtook
the Manſlayer before he got to a
City of Refuge (and in ſome places it was·many miles to one of
them) he might juſtifie the killing
of him.

During the *Iſraelites* ſojourn-
ing in the *Deſert*, the Tabernacle
(where mention is made of the
Altar) was their Refuge in ſuch a
caſe; afterwards in the
Land of (e) *Canaan* there
were ſix Cities of Refuge
appointed, three beyond
Jordan, and three on this
ſide. Three other (f) Ci-
ties of like nature God
promiſed the *Iſraelites*,
upon condition of their
obedience, after their
Coaſts were enlarged; but
it ſeems their *diſobedi-*
ence hindred the accom-
pliſhment thereof, for
Scripture mentioneth not
the fulfilling of it. The
manner of Examination of one
that fled to the City of Refuge
was

(e) Bezer *of the* Reuben-
ites, Ramoth *of* Gilead
of the Gadites, Golan *in*
Baſhan *of the* Manaſſites;
theſe three on this ſide Jordan, Deut.4.41, 43. *theſe*
three appointed by Moſes.
(f) Cadeſh *in* Galilee *in*
Mount Naphtali, Shechem
in Ephraim, *and* Kiria-
tharba *which is in* He-
bron *in the Mountain of*
Judah; *theſe three laſt*
were beyond Jordan, *and*
appointed by Joſhua: Joſh.
20.7. *equally diſtant one*
from another in Canaan.
R. Salom. Jarchi, Deut.
19.3.

was thus; The Confiftory or Bench
of Juftices who lived in that quarter where the Murther was com-
mitted, (*g*) placed the party, be- *(g)* Paul.Fag.
ing brought back from the City *Numb.36. 6.*
of Refuge, in the Court or Judg-
ment Hall, and diligently enquired
and examined the caufe; who, if
he were found guilty of voluntary
Murther, then was he punifhed
with death; but if the fact were
found cafual, then he was fafely
conducted back again to the City
of Refuge, where he enjoyed his
liberty, not only within the Walls
of the City, but within certain
Territories and bounds of the City, within fuch limits until the
death of the High-Prieft (that was
in thofe days) after whofe death
he was at liberty; *Jofh.*20.6. By 20. Jofhua 6.
this means the offender, though he
was not punifhed with death, yet
he lived (for the time, although
the offence was involuntary and
præter intentionem) a kind of
Exile for his own humiliation, and
for the abatement of his wrath who
was

(g) Mafius in Joſh. cap.20. was the Avenger of blood. (d)The *Areopagitæ* had a proceeding a-gainſt *caſual Manſlaughter* , not much unlike, puniſhing the offender ἀπενιαυνσμῷ , with a years baniſhment. It is not agreed amongſt Expoſitors, why the time of this Exilement was limited to the death (h) Aſylum Sanctuarium. In the time of King Henry 8. theſe were places of Sanctuary; All Pariſh Churches,Cathedral and Collegiate Chappels dedicated, and their Churchyards and Sanctuaries to them belonging; and Wells, Weſtminſter, Manchester,Northhampton,Norwich, Darby, and Lancaſter. Afterwards, in the ſame Kings Reign , Mancheſter of the High-Prieſt at that time: but probably thought, that the offender was therefore confined within that City, as within a priſon, during the High-Prieſts life, becauſe the offence did moſt directly ſtrike againſt him, as being amongſt men, ἀρχηϛὸς, *ac Princeps Sanctitatis*, The chief god on earth. Theſe places of Refuge appointed by God, differed from thoſe of *Hercules*, and *Romulus*, and others, Heathens, yea, and Chriſtian Kings formerly of this Nation, becauſe God allowed ſafety only to thoſe who were guiltleſs in reſpect of their intention : but the others were common Sanctuaries (h), as

was determined and Weſtcheſter appointed, Weſtcheſter diſcharged and Stafford appointed, by Letters Pat. from the King. Stamf. fol.116.

well

well for the guilty as the guiltlefs :
If any man did fortuitoufly, or by
chance kill another man, in fuch a
cafe, a Liberty was granted unto
the offender to flie, at firft unto
the Altar for Refuge, as is implied
by that Text of Scripture , *If any
man come prefumptuoufly unto his
Neighbour to flay him with guile,
thou fhalt take him from mine Altar.* Exod.21.14. (*i*).

(i) Thefe places of Sanctuary ex- tended not to Treafon, Wilful Murther, Rape, Burglary, Robbery, Sacriledge, Burning of Houfes and Barns with Corn,&c. 32 H.8.12. 33 H.8.15. It feems they did ex- tend to all thefe offences before thefe Statutes. All Statutes made con- cerning Abjured perfons and Sanctuaries , made before 35 Eliz. were repealed by the 1. of King James c.25. Clergy is fince taken away by feveral Statutes for thofe offences aforefaid , for which Sanctuary by the aforefaid Statutes was taken away.

And it is thought that Temples,
as they were built, had the like
priviledge; as , *Joab fled to the
Temple, and took hold of the horns
of the Altar.* The Reafons why
the Lord appointed Cities of Refuge are principally thefe ; Firft,
left that the Innocent party
might be flain, by the Friends of
him whom he had killed, before
E his

his caufe was heard, and the manner of the flaughter determined by the Judges. Secondly, it was fo appointed, that he might ftay there to the death of the High-Prieft, who was a type of our Bleffed Saviour, by whofe precious death we are all fet free. Thirdly, this was done *ut menti eorum* (*hac ratione*) *medeatur*, &c. to heal and allay the mind and fury of thofe which otherwife would delight in murther; for by his ab-fence and continuance of time, the rage of thofe that fought his life would be qualified, and therefore God provideth, that they fhould not ftill be provoked by the continual fight of him. Fourthly, and further by this, that he that killeth a man unwittingly is appointed to flie, it is fhewed (*quod reus pœnæ efficitur*) that yet he is guilty of fome punifhment. So that involuntary killing was punifhed with a kind of Banifhment among the *Ifraelites:* So likewife amongft the *Athenians*, fuch kind of of Manſlaughter was cenſured with one years Exile. And ſo among the *Iſraelites* , he that eſcaped from the Avenger of blood for it was but an eſcape) was not to go out of the limits and bounds of the City, if he did, it was lawful for the kinſman of the man that was ſlain to kill him.

There is a manifeſt diſtinction of voluntary and involuntary Murther or killing , grounded upon the Law of *Moſes* : Involuntary killing is of two ſorts, there are *ἀτυχήματα*, *chances unlookt for* and *ſudden events* , as when one ſhooteth an Arrow (upon a lawful account , and killeth one unawares, as *Peleus* killed his Son, being in hunting with him. There are beſides theſe , *ἁμαρτήματα* , *errours* and *overſights* , as the Father beateth his Child , purpoſing only to chaſtiſe him , and do him good, and he dieth of it. There are likewiſe two kinds of voluntary or wilful Murther , *ex propoſito* , of *purpoſe* , & *ex impetu animi,*

animi, in *heat* or *rage* ; thefe kind
of Murthers are called ἀδικήματα ,
Iniquities, one may be flain *ex
propofito*, purpofely , *per infidias*,
by lying in wait, when one watch-
eth for the life of a man , and taketh him at advantage , as *Joab*
killed *Abner* , and afterwards fled
to the Temple , and took hold of
the Horns of the Altar, which
notwithftanding could not priviledge him ; and afterwards killed
Amafa , they fufpecting no fuch
thing ; fo *Ifmael* killed *Gedoliah :*
or elfe *per Induftriam* , when one
of fet purpofe picketh quarrels,
and feeketh occafions to provoke
a man that he may kill him. Both
thefe kinds are touched here , *To-
ftat. quæft.* 16. Then one may be
killed in heat and rage when there
was no purpofe before, as *Alexan-
der* the Great killed *Clitus.* This
kind though not fo grievous as the
other, yet is a kind of voluntary
killing , for whom there was no
mercy by Gods Law, as it is in the
Margent of the Great Bible, *Wilful
Murther*

*Murther cannot be pardoned with-
out Gods high difpleafure.* Nay,
as it is more fully in the Text it
felf, *(k) Thine eye* (though the
moft compaffionate fenfe) *fhall not
fpare him, but thou, whoever thou
be, fhalt put away innocent blood
from* Ifrael, *that it may go well
with thee.* Now the putting away
of Innocent blood is by revenging
it on him that fpilt it, as it is in
the 10. v. of the fame Chapter,
*That Innocent blood be not fhed in
the land, which the Lord thy God
giveth thee to inherit, and fo blood
come upon thee;* that is, that the
Blood of the party flain be not im-
puted to thee : This Imputation
of blood, which is of more weight
than the Imputation of all *Adams*
fin, becaufe the command is more
immediate and legible to us;it concerned all the *Ifraelites* in general, but more efpecially doth it
concern thofe chofen by Law to
make Inquifition after *(l)*Innocent

(k) 19.Deut. 13.

(l) Polluitur & fœdatur terra,*Numb.*35. 30.33. *Ye fhall take no fatif-faction for the life of a Mur-therer which is guilty of death, but he fhall be furely put to death; for ye fhall not pollute the Land where-in you are, for blood defileth the Land, and the land cannot be cleanfed of the blood that is fhed therein, but by the blood of him that fhed it.*

blood

blood unlawfully and wilfully fhed as principally Grand Jurors are; for whofe fakes, and that the following difcourfe may fix the better upon their Judgments, and thereby make a right impreffion upon their Confciences to be more circumfpect and careful in their Prefentments in cafes of Blood, I have premifed (as I conceive) what was the will and Law of God (as he himfelf hath declared it, and left it upon Record to us in his Judicials to his people *Ifrael*) who received Laws and Judgments from God himfelf for their whole model and fyftem of Political Government ; agreeable to which I might add the mind of our Saviour Chrift under the Gofpel (who is the beft Interpreter of the Law) in bidding *Peter* put up his Sword (*m*), and his interpretation upon the fixth Command, *He that is angry with his Brother unadvifedly fhall be* culpable *of Judgment* (*n*). I fhall

(*m*) Matt. 26. 52.
(*n*) Matt. 5. 22. *Qui irafcitur his caufa, quan- cum ad velun- tatem homicidi- um fecit,* Chryfoft. hom. in Matt. *Ira eft appetitus ultionis.*

in

in the next place endeavour to ma-
nifeft, how parallel the Laws of
England have been, and are, to the
Judicial Laws of God in the punifhing of Murther and fhedding
Innocent blood, and extending
mercy where it is done *præter intentionem*, unawares and by mif-
fortune, or in the neceffary defence
of a mans own life or property, and
what *Afylum* is provided for fuch;
and how the courfe and practice
of the Laws of *England* ought to
be, in prefenting and making Inquifition (by Grand Jurors) after
the fame.

Not to look fo far back to find
what the Laws were (in cafe of
Felony and Murther) as to the
time of the *Saxons* (o) Heptarchy
in *England*, when the Monarchy
had many heads, being *Bellua
multorum Capitum*; and fo for the
moft part had fo many feveral
Laws, each Prince either pleafing
his own humor, or adapting his
Laws to the condition and quality
of the people he had to govern,

(o) Kent,
South-Saxons,
Weft-Saxons,
Eaft-Saxons,
Eaft-Angles,
Northumber-
land, Mercia.

E 4   which

which as they differed in their
qualities and conftitutions, as much
as the feveral Winds differ the feveral Climates from whence they
blow, out of the four Corners of
the world, from whence many of
their Kingdoms were differenced
and diftinguifhed by names ; fo
did they differ in the nature and
quality of their Laws : fome of
the *Saxon* Kings had excellent
Laws, as *Ina*, as faith Venerable
Bede (*p*), who flourifhed in that
Kings time. The mulct or breach
of Peace was forty fhillings in the
Mercian Law. In the *Weft-Saxon*
Law, fifty fhillings. The punifhment of a Free-man was pecuni-
ary, and lofs of liberty, of a flave
by whipping. Treafon againft the
Lord was Capital, and could not
be appeafed with mony. Amongft
the Laws of *Canutus* the King it
is faid, (*q*) *Si quis in Regia dimi-
caret, Capitale efto, nifi quidem
Rex hoc illi crimen condonarit.*
If any fhould quarrel or fight in
the Kings Palace it was Capital,
except

(*p*)L.7.c.16. &
l.5.c.4.p.375.

(*q*) L.'*Canut.*
fol.117.c.56.

except the King remitted the fault. They were unwilling to put any man to death, becaufe of leffening their ftrength, being fo much divided that for the moft part there was an *æftimatio capitis*, a certain fum of mony, or Corporal punifhment fet upon every Murtherer and Felon, refpecting the quality of the perfon killed, or he that killed him ; yet amongft them there was ftrict inquiry after Blood, by punifhing the offender according to their Laws.

And to look for it amongft the *Danes*, and their Laws, would be to as little purpofe ; for as it is well obferved by Mr. *Lambert* (r), *Temporibus vero Regum* Danorum *fepultum fuit Jus in regno, Leges & Confuetudines, fimul fopitæ, temporibus eorum prava voluntas, vis, & violentia magis regnabant quàm Judicium in terra.* In the time of the *Danifh* Kings, Right was buried, Laws and Cuftomes were laid afleep together, the depraved Will, Strength and Violence

(r) Lambert *L.* Edw. Confeff. c.16. *de Inventione Murdri.*

lence

lence did reign and rule more than Judgment in the land.

Yet to make some amends we have it by good Tradition, that good St. *Edward* the *Confessor*, the last King of the ' *Danes* that was King of *England*) yet of *Saxon* blood, Collected out of the *Danish*, *Saxon*, and *Mercian* Laws, an universal and general Law (whence our Common Law is thought to have had its original)

Ranulph. Cestr. l. 1. c. 550. *Hov.*600. L. *Ed.*c. 35. in *Hoved.*

which may be true of the Written Laws, not of the Customary and unwritten Laws, these being certainly more ancient. Some say, that *Edward* the Third, before

Malmsb. de gest. reg.i.2. c.11.

the Conquest, set forth the Common Law, called the *Laws of Edward* to this day, which St. *Edward* espoused as his Act, and falling last upon the work He carries the name. One says King *Canute* composed our Common Law, which St. *Edward* the *Confessor* observed. This King *Edward* the *Confessor* was in his life of that Holiness, that he received

power

power from above to cure many
Difeafes, amongft others the
fwelling of the Throat (called by
us) *The Kings evil*; a preroga-
tive that continueth hereditary to
his fucceffors, Kings of *England*,
to this day; the powerful effect
whereof hath been moft eminent-
ly manifefted by the Touch of our
moft gracious King that now is K. *CHARLES*
(fince his happy Return into *Eng-* the *Second.*
land) upon very many thoufands;
fome (to my knowledge) that
formerly derided that occult per-
fonal Kingly vertue, inherent to
the Imperial Scepter of *England*,
being of St. *Thomas* his faith, that
would not believe except they
felt, now remaining fully fatisfied
of the truth thereof from their
own experience of the cure upon
themfelves.

The aforefaid St. *Edward*, for
his holinefs, charity, and good
actions, was Canonized for a
Saint, having reigned over *Eng-*
land twenty four years. The Kings
of *England* at this day, in their
Coro-

Coronation Oath taken at the high Altar, fwear efpecially to obferve and keep the Laws of this St. *Edward*. Thefe Laws fo collected by this holy King *Edward*, were by *William* the *Conquerer* (to whom he had bequeathed this Kingdom of *England* by Will, though afterwards he was forced

An.Dom. 1087. to get it by the Sword) confirmed in thefe words, *Hoc quoque præcipio ut omnes habeant & teneant legem Regis* Edwardi *in omnibus rebus*, as Mr. *Lambert* hath it, *inter leges Gulielmi*. Notwithftanding he informs us, that this King *William* (*poft acquifitionem Angliæ*) after he had obtained and fetled the Kingdom in peace, in the fourth year of his Reign,

(s) *Nobilium*. *Concilio* (*s*) *Baronum fuorum*, by the advice of his Nobility, he caufed to be fummoned throughout *England*, the Nobles, Wifemen, and fuch as were skilful in the Laws, Rights and Cuftomes of *England*, and elected twelve Knights out of every County, who

who were sworn before the King
to make a true Collection of the
said Laws and Customes. *Nihil
prætermittentes, nil addentes, nil
prævaricando mutantes.* Amongst
these Laws we do not find Murther punished with death. It being so near the time of the *Danes*
and *Saxons*, it seems he made no
violent alteration of their Laws,
but kept their custome of *æstimatio Capitis*, or Corporal punishment. We find amongst his Laws
these words, (*t*) *Interdico etiam
ne quis occidatur vel suspendatur
pro aliqua culpa sed eruantur ocu-
li, & abscindantur testiculi vel
pedes vel manus, ita quod truncus
vivus remaneat in signum prodi-
tionis & nequitiæ suæ* (*u*). I command that none be killed or hanged for any offence, but that his
eyes be put out, and his Testicles,

(*t*) *Lamb.* inter Leges *Gulielmi* Regis *fol.* 126.

(*u*) By the anci-
ent Law of
England, he
that mahimed
any Man where-
by he lost any
part of his body,
the Delinquent should lose the like part; as he that took away another
mans life should lose his own, Bract.lib.3.numb.4. So if the Defendant in an Appeal of mahime should be found guilty, Judgment a-
gainst the Defendant should have been, That he should lose the like Member that the Plaintiff lost, by this means, a hand for a hand, &c. 40
Ass.9.Mirror c.4 & 5.

or

or feet, or hands be cut off, ſo that
the Trunk of his body may remain alive ; in token of his Treaſon and wickedneſs : any puniſhment then , but loſs of life and
baniſhment , for it is ſaid amongſt
his Laws, *Prohibeo ut nullus ven-
dat hominem extra patriam.* I
forbid that any perſon be ſold out
of his Country.

Now although that theſe kinds
of puniſhments are not commen-
ſurate to the offence , or to the
Law of God , or to the Laws of
England, in caſes of Murther,
there being not life for life ; yet
who is there almoſt amongſt the
Sons of men , that would not rather chuſe to be hanged , than
to have his eyes put out , his
Teſticles, feet, and hands cut off,
and to ſurvive with ſuch a brand
of Ignominy. (*x*) Amongſt the
Laws of the Conquerer , in the
Title *Lex Murdrorum*, it is there
found ; If any be found Murthered, the Village in whom he was
ſo found , was within eight days

(*x*) *Lamb.* in
leges *Edvardi*
R.c.15. Lex
Murdrorum.
v.*Stamf.*lib.1.
fol.17.

to

to deliver the Murtherer; *Justi-cia Regis*; if he were not found within one Month and a day, the Village was to pay forty marks; if the Village were not able, then the Hundred was to pay it, and this mony was to be fealed up, under the Seal of a Nobleman of the County, and fent into the Exchequer, there to remain a year and a day, to the end, that if the Hundred or Village could within a year and a day bring the body of the Murtherer to Juftice, they fhould have their mony again; if they could not within that time take him, the Parents of him that was murthered fhould have fix mark, and the King the reft; if he had no Parents, then his Lord or Mafter fhould have it; if no Lord or Mafter, then (*y*) *Se-lagus ejus*, i.e. *fide cum eo ligatus*, that is, his Pledge or Surety; if he had none of thefe, then the King fhould have all the forty Marks (which was as much then as five hundred pounds now) *fub*

cujus

(*y*) His Pledge or Surety.

cujus protectione, & pace degunt universi; If the Murtherer were found, and would not defend his Innocency, *Judicio Dei*, *scilicet aqua, vel ferro,* that is, stand in hot scalding-water, or pass barefoot over hot-bars of Iron, *fieret de eo Justitia,* let Justice be executed upon him; but what this Justice was, or what punishment he should suffer, some doubt there is: (*z*)Some say it was *ad voluntatem Regis,* or the usual way of *æstimatio Capitis,* or Corporal punishment, and not to suffer death, because (as before is observed) there is found amongst those Laws, *Ne quis occidatur, vel suspendatur, pro aliqua Culpa;* though others are of another Judgment, that it was Capital if the King pleased, whatever the punishment was; you shall not read of any Insurrection or Rebellion before the Conquest, when the view of Frank-pledge, and other

(*χ*) *That is, so much as one paid for the killing of a man; by which it appeareth, that. such Government was in those days, as slaughters of men were most rarely committed, as Mr.* Lambert *collecteth.* Lamb. Expositio verb. *Estimatio.* Flet. *lib.*1. *c.*42. Hoved. *fol.*344.

other ancient Laws of this Realm were in their right ufe.

There are many that are full of Sr. *Thomas Moore's* kindnefs, and think it too much that a man fhould lofe his life for crimes under Murther, as for Theft, &c. (but none fo kind to a Murtherer) for which anciently a lofs of a Hand, Eye, Leg, or other member was in ufe; yet the party taken in the manner, *hand habend.* having the ftoln thing in his hand, in his poffeffion, might be killed amongft the *Saxons*, he could not buy his Crime out; and the *Spanifh* condemning to the Gallies, is thought by fome the only way. Mr. *Daniel* will have it, that *as yet* (writing of King *Henry* the Second's time) *they came not fo far as Blood*, which is not fo; for King *Henry* the Firft (*a*) (abrogating the *were-gilde*) by which a man might have bought out his offence, made a Law, fays *Hoveden*, *Ut fi quis in furto*

(*a*) Hoveden *faw.* 471. *in* H.I. *Concil.* Birghamftead. *Concil.*197.*L.K.*Canut.*c.*6:. *L.K.*Ina 5.37. Æthelft.

F

furto vel latrocinio deprehenſus fuiſſet ſuſpenderetur ; to hang the Thief : with whom *Vigormenſis* and *Rad. Niger* agree. And the Lo. *Coke* obſerves in the third *Inſtitutes* , that before the Reign of King *Henry* the Firſt the Judgment for Felony was not alwaies the ſame , but King *Henry* the Firſt ordained by Parliament, that the Judgment for all manner of Felonies ſhould be , that *he ſhould*

9 H. 1.

be hanged by the neck until he be

Matth. Pariſ.
continuat.
1005.

dead : After , in the latter end of the Reign of King *Henry* the Third, we find a Thief who had ſtoln twelve Oxen beheaded. Capital puniſhments have not only been in uſe againſt Homicides and Felonies , but other Tranſgreſſors alſo , and amongſt thoſe who worſhipped God rightly (as is well obſerved) we meet with no Divine precept before *Judah*, which makes Whoredom worthy of death, yea, when he is told , Tamar *thy Daughter in law hath played the Harlot* , he anſwers ;

Bring

Bring her forth and let her be burnt. (*b*) Amongſt the *Bri-tains*, if the Wife killed her Husband ſhe was to be burnt ; ſo are the *Engliſh* Laws to this day. *We may proceed* (ſays *Grotius*) *by conjecture of the Divine will, with the help of Natural reaſon, from like to like, and that which is a Law againſt Felonies and Murthers, may be extended to others as dangerouſly miſchievous : It is a hard diſpute, whether there be more mercy in death, or putting out of Eyes, cutting off Legs, Arms, &c. or in the Gallies. It is believed, that the boldneſs and number of Malefactors begot the Law of death, and thoſe whom Death with ſo much Infamy (ſo often reiterated before their eyes) cannot fright, will never think any Torment whatſoever (where life is left them, though with more miſery th⸻ be ſpoken) ter-rible*

(*b*) Cæſar's *Comment.l. 6. ante Chriſtum natum* 1600 *annis.*

F 2   It

It is well obſerved by the Lo.

Coke 3. In-
ſtit. Epilog.

Coke, that, *Videbis ea ſæpe committi, quæ ſæpe vindicantur.* Thoſe offences are often commit‑ ted, that are often puniſhed ; and he gives his Reaſon for it, That the frequency of the puniſhment makes it ſo familiar, as it is not feared. *For Example* (ſaith he) *what a lamentable caſe it is, to ſee ſo many Chriſtian men and*

Sta. perlege
plot.

women ſtrangled on that curſed Tree of the Gallows, inſomuch, as if in a large field a man might ſee together all the Chriſtians, that but in one year, throughout Eng‑ land, *come to that untimely and ignominious death, if there were any ſpark of Grace, or Charity in him, it would make his heart to bleed for pity and compaſſion.* I my ſelf have known at one Aſſizes in the County of *Monmouth*, where one hath had Judgment to die for ſtealing a Horſe, and Re‑ prieved, in order to procure his Pardon ; another narrowly ac‑ quitted of a Felony, and made uſe

use of by the Goaler, to be the
Common-Hangman at the same
Assizes; that both these persons
(the one breaking the Goal, the
other having his liberty, as being
acquitted) were both taken in
one Felony and Burglary before
the next Assizes, committed to
the Goal, and received Judgment
of death, and were both hanged
together. So little doth favour,
terrour, or example work a Re-
formation upon those that are
hardened in their sins, and want
grace to make good use of
them.

But it is thought horrible and
grievous, that a mans life (the
life of a Christian) or any of the
Members of his body, should be
taken away for so small a value
as thirteen pence (I take twelve
pence to be but petit Larceny,
for which he shall be whipt) it is
very plain that the Statute of 3*Ed.* 3 Ed.1.15.
1. *c.* 15. declaring what Prisoners
are Mainprizable, or Barable, says
amongst other offences (*viz.*) or
F 3   *for*

for Larceny, which amounteth not above the value of twelve pence: nay, for lefs. King *Æthelftanes* Laws begin with Thieves, and fpeak thus; *Firft, that a man fpare no Thief who is in the manner, having in his hands taken above eight pence* (it feems eight pence then was in the nature of a Petit Larceny;) a Ram in the *Saxons* time was worth but four pence: that which was heretofore fold for twelve pence, would now be worth forty fhillings.

In the Affize of Bread (long after the *Saxons*) in the 51*th* of *H.* 3. eight Bufhels of Wheat are valued but at twelve pence. In *Edward* the Third's time a Bufhel of Wheat was but ten pence; a Haymaker had but a penny a day, Reapers of Corn two pence, an Acre to be mowed for five pence, Threfhing a quarter of Wheat or ie but two pence, a Mafter-`arpenter three pence a day, and ıis man two pence, a Free Mafon `ur pence, others three pence, their

their Boys one penny, Plaifterers
and their Knaves (fo named in
the Act) the fame manner, and
to find themfelves meat and
drink. See the Statute 25 *E.* 3. 25 Ed.3.c.1,3.
c. 1, and 3. And by the Statute
made the *6th* of *H.* 8. of much
later time, the wages of a Bayliff
of Husbandry was but fixteen
fhillings eight pence, and for
Cloathing him five fhillings with
meat and drink, a Chief Hinde or
Shepherd twenty fhillings, and
for his Cloathing five fhillings,
every Common Servant fixteen
fhillings eight pence,for Cloathing
four fhillings, no Woman Servant above ten. fhillings, her
Cloathing four fhillings, and no
Mafter might have given more.

And although *twelve pence*
keeps not the old Rate, but the
Modern, yet things are prized in
trials of Life far below their
worth, and no man lofeth his life
(in a fingle and fimple Felony)
but where the thing ftoln rifeth
to more than many twelve pences
F 4   (efpecially

(especially after the Old estimate)
but indeed the quality of the Offender, circumstances of the offence, and of the times, are main-
ly considerable in our Law, where
any mans life is taken away in
such a Felony.

But to return to our proper
Subject, and to manifest what the
Laws of *Engl ind* were (in Cases
of blood) not long after the Conquerer, and how tender a regard
the Law of *England* (answerable
to the Law of God) had of the
Life of man. By a Canon of our
Old *English* Church, he that killed
a Man in publick war (though justifiable) was enjoyned a
Penance of forty days.
(*c*) By the Common Law
killing by misadventure,
unawares, or in a mans own defence was Murther, founded upon
the Judicial Law, before the Cities of Refuge; and the forfeiture
and punishment of both was, as in
case of Murther, as appears plainly by the Statutes of *Marlebridge*
and

*Concil.*Saxon. 383.

(*c*) Misadventure *at the Common Law adjudged* Murther, Stamf. *fol.*16.*c.*8.

and *Gloucefter*; the Forfeiture of
Goods and Chattels remains as
yet : The words of the Statute of
Marlebridge 52 *H.* 3. are as fol- 52 H. 3.
loweth, *Murther from henceforth
fhall not be adjudged before our
Juftices where it is found Mif-
fortune only*; which fhews, before
that Statute though a man were
killed by Misfortune, he had the
fame Judgment in Law as for
Murther : So that after the making of that Statute until the *6th*
of *Edw.* 1. Writs were granted 6 Ed. 1.
of courfe, where there was a furmife that the man was killed by
Misfortune, or, *fe defendendo*, or
in any other manner, where the
killing was not Felony, and
thereupon a Pardon of courfe, or
Grace, was granted to the party,
who only forfeited his Goods and
Chattels, and by benefit of that
Pardon, had only his liberty out of
prifon, which without he could
not have.

This

This way of Mercy it feems did
ftretch too far, and covered too
many guilty perfons (as I fear
yet it does) under her wings,
when as their feveral Cafes were
not judicially examined, indicted,
and tried, before hand, by a
Grand Jury, and a Jury of Life
and Death before a Learned Judge
(as in ordinary Trials of Criminals) whereby it came to pafs
that many Murthers and Manflaughters efcaped under the fa-
vourable furmife of a *per infortunium*, or *fe defendendo*, as if it
were done by misfortune, or in
his own defence, and fo came off
from a foul Murther by a Pardon
of Courfe. Now for. remedy in
this cafe came the Statute of
Gloucefter; the words of which

6 Ed.1.c.9.　Statute are as followeth;

*The King commandeth, that no
Writ fhall be granted out of
Chancery for the death of a man,
to enquire, whether ·a man did
kill another by Misfortune, or in
his own defence, or in any other
manner*

*manner, without Felony; but he
shall be put in prison until the
coming of the Justices in Eyre, or
Justices assigned to the Gaol-
delivery, and shall put himself
upon the Country before them for
good and evil* (that is, for life or
death;) *if in case it be found by
the Country that he did it in his
defence, or by misfortune; Then
by the Report of the Justices to
the King, the King shall take him
to his Grace (if it please him.)*
The Report to the King is, to
Certifie the Record into the Chancery, where the King is alwaies
present; and therefore it is called
a *Pardon of Course*, Stamford *fo.* 15. Stamf. *fol.*15.
whereas the Kings own *hand* and
fiat is to other Pardons. So that
here it is very plain, that he that
will be acquitted and discharged
out of Prison for Manslaughter,
per infortunium, or *se defendendo*
(*ex Gratia Regis*) must first put
himself, *super Patriam*, upon the
Country *de bono & malo* (the very
words of the Act) and that is
upon

upon a Jury of Life and Death;
and this he cannot do except the
Grand Jury find the Bill of Indictment, Murther or Manslaughter, let the matter of fact be
what it will; for if the Grand
Jury shall but find the truth of
the fact, as it appears in evidence
to them, or from their own
knowledge (which is that which
they now so much stand upon,
that is the very special matter
that makes it Manslaughter, by
misfortune or *se defendendo*) the
party can never come to be Arraigned upon such an Indictment,
for that is not Felony, and if he
shall be charged with it (the
Grand Jury having only found the
special matter in the Indictment
or Inquisition) the party must
either plead *guilty*, or *not guilty*,
either confess and justifie the Fact,
or deny it; if he confess, he
cannot Justifie it, for mens lives
are so precious in the eye of the
Law, that the death of a man
cannot be Justified, except in course
of

of Juftice, in a lawful War, or in a juft defence of a mans life and property, againft fuch as would rob, or defignedly murther him. The Defendant in Appeal cannot Juftifie the death of a man at his own fuit, *fe defendendo*, but muft plead *not guilty*. Nay, a Verdict of the Jury of Life and Death, that *A* killed *B fe defendendo*, or *per Infortunium*, is no good Verdict; the fpecial matter muft be fet down in writing by them, that the Court may judge the killing to be upon inevitable neceffity; neither Grand Jury that hears but one fide, nor Jury of Life and Death (that hear both fides) are Judges in this cafe. For, upon the fpecial matter found by the Jury of Life and Death, if the Court fhall not adjudge that fpecial matter good in Law to acquit him of Murther or Manflaughter, it may be either murther or manflaughter in him, and the party may be hanged notwithftanding fuch Verdict of the Jury of Life and

Br. *Appeal* 122.

Coron. 302.

43. *lib.* Aff. *p.* 31.

Stamf. *lib.* 3. *c.* 9. *fol.* 165.

and Death, how can the Court be judge of the matter in Law, when they hear not the matter in fact from the Witnesses on both sides, and the Parties defence for himself, which they can never do, if the Grand Jury shall take upon them (as they presume they may) to find the Special matter themselves, whereby the Party cannot be Arraigned, that so he may put himself *de bono & malo super patriam*, as the Statute of *Gloucester* before-mentioned especially requires. If the Party charged with such an Indictment from the Grand Jury (where they will find only the Special matter) shall confess it, when he is charged with it (as sure he may) then the Evidence can never be heard in Court, whereby the Judge may determine the point in Law, whether the offence upon the whole matter be Murther or Manslaughter, or as they find it, and that is meer matter of Law, whether *super totam materiam* of the Evidence (and

(and that muſt be Evidence on
both ſides) it be murther, Manſlaughter in general, Manſlaughter
upon the Statute *per Infortunium*,
ſe defendendo, juſtifiable as againſt
a Thief, or *in loco & tempore belli*;
and how exceeding dangerous and
inconvenient were it for Grand
Jurors, ſo far to anticipate the
Judgment of the Court, and to
take upon themſelves (upon the
hearing only of Witneſſes on one
ſide, and perhaps not all of them
neither) the ſole Judgment of Law
in all theſe Caſes, by not finding
the Indictment (which is but the
Kings Declaration for the loſs of
his Subject, in the ſame manner as
it is adviſed by the Kings Council
Ingroſſed, ſworn in Court, and
delivered to them) eſpecially (for
that is alwaies intended) where
they have probable Evidence (for
they need no more) to prove ſuch
a perſon killed by the hands of
ſuch a perſon, ſuch a day, year,
and place. Nay, by the Statute of
Gloucaſter, they muſt either find
the

the Indictment in such a case Murther, for all Indictments (about the
killing of a man) were so before
that Statute, and no Law since to
alter it, or the party can never
have a *Certiorari* out of Chancery
for his Pardon of Course, whereby
he may be discharged out of Prison; for by the strictness of Law,
he ought to remain in Prison without Bail until his pardon be procured, which Pardon saves not his
Goods or personal Estate, but only
pardons his Offence, his violation
of the King's Peace (which is violated in the loss of a Subject) according to the Statute of *Glouce-*
ster, and procures his liberty, and
discharge out of Prison.

The words contained in the Writ
of *Certiorari* out of Chancery, in
order to the obtaining of a Pardon
of Grace, and removing the Record into Chancery, that there the
King may see by the Record the
truth and nature of the offence, according to the Statute of *Glouce-*
ster, being well observed make it
very

very plain, that the Special matter of Fact muſt be found by the ſecond Jury, the Jury of Life and Death, and which is ſo ſuggeſted in Chancery before the Iſſuing forth of ſuch Writ, as by the Writ more fully appears, viz. *Quia ut accepimus, quòd A. B. indictatus, & per Inquiſitionem patriæ compert. extitiſſet, quod idem A interfecit prædict. C. ſe def. & non per feloniam aut malitiam præcogitat. unde dictus A. Gaol. noſtr. prædict. remiſſ.eſt ad gratiam noſtram inde expectand. nos ea de cauſa ſuper tenor.Record. & proceſſ. Inquiſitionis præd. Certiorari volentes, vobis mandamus quod ſi ita eſt, tunc tenor. Record. pro proceſſ. prædict. cum omnibus ea tangent. in Cancell. noſtram ſub ſigillis veſtris diſtincte & aperte mittatis.* Obſerve how this ancient Writ complies with, and explains the Statute of *Glouc.* in this caſe; here is in it *Indictatus*, that is, by the Grand Jury, and *per Inquiſitionem patriæ compert. extitiſſet*, that is, the Jury of Life

G and

Certiorary out of Chancery.

and Death; for that is the only Trial in our Law, by the Country, *per Patriam*; and whoever is tried by that Jury, *posuit se de bono & malo super patriam*, which must be for Felony and Murther, the very words of the Statute; for this Jury is to find, in their Writ, that it was *se defendendo & non per felon. aut malitiam præcogitat.* as it is in the Verdict; and observe by the Writ, he is not to be discharged out of Gaol before his pardon of Course procured, for it is in the Writ, *Gaol. nostræ præd. remiss.est* (it seems he was there before) *ad gratiam nostr. inde expectand. &c.* and further, observe the *Mandamus* in this Writ (*si ita est*) if it be so, that the Offence hath received such a trial by two Juries, then Certifie the Record, otherwise not; and what Judge that doth not truly understand this (*si ita est*) which he can never truly do from a Grand Jury, will Certifie such a Record in Chancery, to the King himself, in Cases of Blood.

By

By this it may appear, to all that are rational and unprejudiced, that have not formerly afferted the contrary Opinion, and therefore like the Opiniators of this Age, will (for no other reafon) maintain it, That Grand Jurors are not left fo free herein, to find what they pleafe, or as they would have it, ftrictly according to their Evidence, as the Gentlemen of thefe latter times have taken upon them to do, and even to ftand upon it, againft the Learned Judges themfelves, and their Directions and Advice. Befides, how greatly do they injure the party accufed; for if he be Guilty of no higher an Offence than Manflaughter *per Infortunium*, or *fe Defendendo*, and the Grand Jury will not find it Murder, whereby he may put himfelf (as the Statute of *Gloucefter* directs, *de bono & malo fuper patriam*) he can never by a pardon of courfe, receive a total and final difcharge from the faid Offence. For if he fhould be Indicted at any

time again of Murder for the
death of that Party (as he may
be at any time after, during his
life, notwithftanding fuch pardon,
where it was not found Murder
or Manflaughter at the firft) he
can make no Plea to fuch Indictment, in difcharge of it: he cannot plead *auter foits* Acquit, or
Convict, or Attaint of the fame
Offence, becaufe he never put himfelf *de bono & malo fuper patriam*,
upon his Country, his life was never in hazard for it: whereas, if he
have been once prefented by the
Grand Jury for Murder, and thereupon Arraigned, received a full
Tryal, and according to the Statute of *Gloucefter*, had been acquitted of the Murder, and the
fpecial matter of *per Infortunium*,
or *fe Defendendo* found in their
Verdict (which by the Law ought
to be fo found by the Jury of Life
and Death) under their Hands,
that the Judge (upon hearing the
whole matter) may be fatisfied
it is found according to Evidence
given

given in Court, and thereupon adjudge what that Offence is in Law. If in this cafe the party that hath received fuch a full Tryal, and hath fued out a *Certiorari* out of Chancery; and upon the Return of that, hath had the Special matter, the whole Record of proceedings certified by the Judge, before whom the Record remains, and thereupon hath procured his pardon of courfe out of Chancery; fuch perfon can never be called in queftion again for the fame Offence, but he may plead that Record and Verdict of Acquittal from the Murder or Manflaughter, notwithftanding it might happen to be proved afterwards either Murder or Manflaughter, it fhall difcharge and acquit him for ever.

And if the Grand Jury (as in this cafe) ought to find every *per Infortunium* Murder (notwithftanding by the Evidence it appear no more to them) *à multo fortiori*, they ought to find every

Offence

Offence (that appears to them upon Evidence to be but Manslaughter) Murder. For the (*d*) *Bill* of Indictment, as it comes from their hands, is but the Kings Declaration of the matter of Fact, to which the Prisoner may plead, *Not Guilty*; and joyn Iſſue with the King, and have it tryed, Whether he be Guilty, or not? *modo & forma*, as it is laid in the Indictment, or may confeſs and juſtifie, as he ſhall find cauſe. For this Indictment or Preſentment of the Grand Jury in the behalf of the King againſt the Priſoner, ſets forth an Act done, *Vi & Armis*, againſt the Kings Peace, his Crown, and Dignity, all which are violated, diſhonoured, & weakned in the loſs of a Subject, in the ſhedding of Innocent Blood, by which his Land is defiled, and his Laws violated; and this according to the Laws of God and Man (*prima facie*) may be Murder, and therefore ought

(*d*) *As in the two Houſes of Parliament it is but a Bill whilſt in their hands, the Royal aſſent makes it an Act. So it is but a Bill in the Grand Jury's hand, the other Jury makes it an Act.*

as

as well(as all Declarations at Law)
to be fet forth in the fulleft circumftances of aggravation a Fact of
Blood (which far exceeds all other
Facts) will bear, efpecially in lay-
ing the ground work and foundation of the Charge, becaufe it cannot heighten or increafe, but may
leffen and decreafe, like the Moon
in the full, to its loweft wane, e-
ven to nothing, upon a full Examination and Debate of the whole
matter, by hearing of Parties and
Witneffes on both fides, and receiving in the face and audience of
the Court fuch a fcrutiny and nar-
row fearch (as blood requires) into all circumftances and aggravations of the Offence, that are laid in
the Indictment, by the Learned
Judge (who is of Counfel as well
for the Prifoner as the King, and
muft not let the Prifoner fuffer for
want of Counfel in Law) that a
Grand Jury cannot poffibly do,
they hearing but only Witneffes on
one fide, and not the Prifoner;
befides their want of Judgment

G 4   and

and Knowledge in the Law in all Cafes of Blood: whereas, if the Grand Jury·fhall take upon them (which they ought not to do) to put out of the Indictment and Declaration of the King, the words *Ex malitia præcogitata*) the only words that make it Murder, the Court can never Judicially examine the malice, which is commonly a fecret latent thing, carried on with a great privacy and cunning, and appears not in all cafes of Murder exprefs, (and no Evidence can prove further to a Grand Jury) whereas the Law in many cafes implies a malice to make it Murder (although the Parties never faw or heard of each other before) which lies not in proof of Witneffes, but arifeth as a point of Law upon the circumftances of the Fact, which, not a Grand Jury, but the Court is Judge of, being matter of Law, which Judgment in Law is wholly fruftrated and taken from the Court, when the Grand Jurors

put

put out thefe words, *Ex malitia
præcogitata,* which only make it
Murder, out of the Indictment.
And by fuch favour, indulgence, or wilfulnefs in Grand Jurors, many times the greateft
Murder efcapes by a *per Infortunium,* *fe Defendendo,* or at
leaft by a Manflaughter. For if
the Grand Jurors fhall only find
it Manflaughter, the Prifoner upon his Arraignment, prefently
(if he can but read, get any one
to help him, or corrupt the Ordinary, no great difficulty to do)
confeffes the Indictment, and
prevents all further tryal upon
that Offence, and fo neither the
Judge, nor Court, can ever come
to underftand (although there be
twenty Witneffes againft the Prifoner) what Evidence the Grand
Jury had to find it no higher than
Manflaughter; nor fhall ever come
judicially to examine the nature,
quality, or malice (if any be)
circumftances, and truth of the
Fact, although in it felf the foul-
eft

eſt Murder that can be (as my own above Forty years experi-ence, attending the Crown Court in one Circuit under many Learn-ed Judges, hath too often experi-enced) together with the com-mon practice of labouring Grand Jurors to ſuch a Preſentment, and contriving with the Priſoner to confeſs the Manſlaughter, left the truth and foulneſs of the Murder ſhould too clearly manifeſt it ſelf (as truth ever will) upon a Ju-dicial, faithful, and careful Exa-mination of the Fact by the Learn-ed Judge, upon hearing the Par-ty, and Evidence on both ſides.

4 H. 4. 2.
37 H. 8. 8.
It is true (as appears by two ſeveral Acts of Parliament noted in the Margent) that at the making of thoſe Acts there was a complaint in Parliament, That Indictments were ſtuffed with more words than the Of-fence required, and that of pur-poſe to aggravate the Offence more than it was grievous in it ſelf.

self. For as it is well observed
by Mr. *Poulton, That the circum-*
stances of every Offence do aug-
ment or diminish it according to
the qualities thereof. And by
those two Acts of Parliament it
may be observed there was a re-
formation and redress made therein, by leaving out some formal
aggravating words (but then material) used in those times in all
Indictments of Felony and Murther, as by the Statute of the
4th of *H.* 4. 2. the words then con-
stantly used in all Indictments of
Felony (without which the Indictments were not good) were
[*Insidiatores viarum & depopu-*
latores agrorum) provides that
those words should be left out in
all such Indictments, and yet the
Indictments should be good without them: And well they might
leave them out; for how useless
and impertinent (as to the Ef-
fence of the Indictment) were
those words, and yet the effect
of them must be still observed. As
alfo

(e) Poulton *de*
Pace Regis &
Regni, fol. 167.

4 H. 4. 2.

also by the Statute of the 37 *H.*
8. *c.* 8. the words, *Vi & Armis,*
viz. cum baculis, cultellis, ar-
cubus & fagittis, or such other
like words (before time commonly used and comprifed in all Indictments and Inquifitions of Treafon, Murther, Felony, Trefpafs,
and other Criminal Offences)
fhall not of neceffity (for they
were fo before) be put or comprifed in any Inquifition or Indictment; but it fhall be good
only with thefe words (*Vi & Ar-*
mis, &c.) leaving out the other a-
gainft any advantage that may be
taken (as formerly it was) by
Writ of Error, Plea, or otherwife;
for thefe words were to very little
purpofe, to be of neceffity ufed in
every Indictment : For as to fome
Indictments, there could be nothing of pertinency or congruity
to the Offence in them. And
yet let it here be obferved by the
way, That in thofe times, and
before thofe Statutes formerly
mentioned, continually (in all
In-

Indictments) thofe words were
ufed, and the Indictments found
by the Grand Jurors , without a-
ny proof made to them of fuch
circumftances (then effential) as
[*Infidiatores viarum* , *depopula-*
tores agrorum] liers in wait to de-
ceive upon the High-ways , and
deftroyers of Husbandry ; or, as in
the other Statute , *Cum baculis,*
cultellis , *arcubus & fagittis* ,
viz. with Staves, Knives , Bows
and Arrows ; when perhaps he
that committed the Offence had
not one of thefe Weapons about
him , or was guilty of the leaft
of thefe circumftances of Aggravation , which were then held
neceffary to every Indictment ;
which fhews how obfervable (at
that time) Grand Jurors were to
the directions of the Court ,.and
to the Kings Council , in drawing the Indictments and Circumftances of it , Whether fuch Circumftances lay in proof, or no ?
But in neither of thefe Statutes,
nor any other Statute , is there
any

any Exceptions made to thefe words, in any Indictment for the killing of a man (*Ex malitia præcogitata*) then ufed in all Indictments for the killing of any perfon unlawfully, which (as is faid before) are of great confe-quence and ufe to be put into all Indictments againft any per-fon that hath fhed innocent blood. For, as Mr. *Poulton*, in the very Folio before quoted, faith, (f) (writing upon the two former Statutes laft mentioned;) *If one be Indicted of Murther or Man-flaughter, there muft be of necef-fity in the Indictment, a ftroke fuppofed, viz. tali die, & anno felonicè, & ex malitia præcogi-tata interfecit & murdravit.* Here it is plain, that the Indict-ment of Manflaughter, as well as Murther, muft have thefe words, *Ex malitia*, &c. in it. Neither let any think that it is preft further, *in foro legis*, than it will bear *in foro confcientiæ*; or that by this means Grand Jurors are ufed but

as

(f) Poulton *de Pace, &c.* *fol.167.*

Poult. *ut fupra,* 1. m. Dier. 59.

as Cyphers (like the Ordinary at
the Affizes) *pro forma tantum* ,
and that the Arguments of Law
and Reafon here ufed , feem'd to
perfwade them (like thofe of
the Church of *Rome*) to be of
an implicite Faith , to believe as
their Leaders would have them ,
and to do as they require them,
and yet to be under the Obligation of an Oath to prefent the
truth of the matter of Fact. It is
far otherwife (being rightly confidered) they are not fworn to
try the whole truth of the Offence , fo as nothing may be altered in what they find , for then
there would be no need of another
Jury ; they are neither to convict the Party , nor determine the
Law, Whether it be Murther or
Manflaughter ? or of what kind
or *Species* it is , as it appears to
them upon the hearing of but one
fide, and that but. of Witneffes ,
not of the Party, that is left (as
is faid before). to the fecond Jury , who are properly Tryers of
the

the Offence *de vicineto*) of the very Neighbourhood; not Inquirers only (as Grand Jurors from every part of the County) where Parties, and Witneſſes, and Council, on both ſides (if occaſion be) may be lawfully heard.

(g) *Jurato creditur in Judicio. And to ſay the truth*, ſaith the Lord *Coke, we never read in any Act of Parliament , ancient Author, Book-caſe, or Record, that in* Criminal Ca*ſes, the party accuſed ſhould not have witneſſes ſworn for him , and therefore there is not ſo much as* Scintilla Juris *againſt it.* Cok. 3. Inſt. fol. 79.

(g) The Grand Jury are only ſworn to inquire, and true preſentment make of all ſuch things and matters as ſhall be given them in charge, to preſent nothing for malice, &c. nor leave any thing unpreſented for favour,&c. From hence often Grand Jurors frame an Argument to themſelves, that it is part of their Oath to preſent all ſuch things as ſhall be given them in charge, that generally the Judges in their charges dilate upon the ſeveral *Species* and differences in Murther : As , what Offence the Law makes Murther ? what Manſlaughter at Common Law? what upon the Statute? what

what *per Infortunium*? what *fe Defendendo*? what is malice ex-preffed? and what is malice im-plied; and therefore wherever they find thefe fpecifical differ-ences by their Evidence, they are fo to prefent it, and not other-wife.

This is upon a great miftake, nor is it, or can it be fo intended by the Judges; for although it is true that the Judges (for the moft part, not all of them) in their charges to the Grand Jury (which I humbly conceive were better omitted) do, ufually menti-on and branch out the feveral fpecifical differences and diftincti-ons the Books of Law make in fhedding of Blood, in Murther, and Manflaughter, I conceive, more to inform the whole Coun-try, and to fhew their Learning, and the Law therein, than inten-tionally that the Grand Jury fhould prefently (fome of them perhaps never ferving before, *uno intuitu*) take it into the confide-

H ration

ration of their Oath , and make it
the nice Duty of their Inquiry ,
which indeed . they can never at-
tain unto , or determine the Law
therein , by only hearing of an
Accufation of one fide , from
which they are only to prepare
fit matter for the Court to proceed further upon , and to make
a more diligent inquiry after.
Such diftinctions and directions
from the Judge being much more
proper for a Jury of Life and
Death , when any Queftion of
Blood comes before them to be
confidered of , and to be tryed and
determined , who have the only
means to do it , by hearing all
Parties, all Evidence on both fides;
as alfo the directions of the Court,
as to the quality and nature of
the Offence, to give them a true
light to make a right diftinction
therein.

Finch 25. *Cafe*
of prefentment
and Indictment.

It is well faid by a Learned
Writer of the Law; *An Indict-*
ment is an Inquiry finding fome
Offence againft the King. It was
the

the *Kings Action whereupon the
Party shall be Arraigned*, or put
to *Answer by the King*, and *tryed by another Jury.* . *Every strong
suspicion of such an Offence, though
it be in case of Felony appearing
of Record, hath the force of an
Indictment*, as in an *Action of
Trespass for Goods carried away;
if the Defendant plead, Not Guilty, and be found Guilty,
he is a Felon, &c.* (*h*)
*So in an Appeal of Mur-
ther, if the Plaintiff, after Declaration be Non-
suit, the King shall pro-
ceed upon that Appeal, as upon an
Indictment found*: So He. And as
it is in (*i*) *Doctor* and
Student ; The Grand Ju-
ry is only charged with
the effect of the Bill (*viz.*) whether he be guilty of the Felony or
Murther in the Indictment, within
the Shire, and not whether he be
guilty, *modo & forma,* as in the
Bill is specified. And so when
they say *Billa vera*, they say tru-

(*h*) *In ancient time it
was usual to Arraign one
taken in the manner with-
out any Appeal or Indict-
ment.*

(*i*) *Doctor & Student,
lib.2.cap. Abridgment.*

ly (as they take the effect of the
Bill to be) so it is though the Bill
vary from the day, year, and place,
so it vary not from the Shire; as
if there were false Latin in the
Bill they might well say, *Billa
vera*, for their Verdict stretcheth
but to the Felony, not to the truth
of the Latin.

There is very much difference
in Law betwixt an Inquiry and a
Trial, betwixt a Presentment and
a Conviction; besides, the Judges
do now give it in charge to the
Grand Jurors, and so part of their
duty (if not of their Oath) that
when they have such an Indictment of Murther come to their
hands, if they find upon their E-
vidence, that the party said to be
slain in the Indictment, by the
person there charged with it, with
the time, and place, and manner
how, they are to enquire no farther into the nature of it (what
offence this is in Law) but to find
it as it stands in the Indictment,
which (for ought they know, upon

on a further and more clear dif-
cuffion of it in Court) may appear
as full, as it is laid in the Indictment ; however it paffeth fairly
out of their hands, they may
more clearly than *Pilate* wafh
their hands in Innocency from the
Innocent blood of fuch a perfon,
and very well difcharge their
Oath, the Law, and a good Confcience, letting it pafs from them
with the Indorfment of *Billa vera*, a Bill that hath truth in it, fit
to be confidered further by the
Court and another Jury.

And as Indictments at the Kings
Suit do fucceed Appeals, at the
parties Suit, fo ought they to be
drawn and prefented as large and
as full for the King, as an Appeal
of death for the party, which e-
ver was for Murther (if the party
Appellant would fo have it) and
that may very reafonably be ap-
plied to Indictments that the
Statute of *Gloucefter* directs in
Appeals, *viz.* That no Appeal
fhall be abated fo foon, as they

have been heretofore : But if the Appellant in an Appeal do declare the Deed, the year, the day, the hour, the time of the King, and the Town where the Deed was done, and with what weapon he was flain, the Appeal fhall ftand in effect.

6 E. 1. 9.

Now fo great an exactnefs of the year, day, and hour, is not required in an Indictment, as in an Appeal (being the only violent profecution of the party) in favour of life, many Niceties were ftood upon more than in other Actions. And Mr. Juftice *Stamford* fays, A man is not of neceffity compellable at Common Law at this day, to put into his Declaration the hour; the day was neceffary to be put down in an Appeal; for if the Appellee can prove by certain Demonftrations and Teftimony of credible Witneffes, that he was the fame day at another place, at fuch a diftance as it was not poffible for him to be there the day of the committing

ting of the fact, or twenty miles off the same hour the murther was committed, the Appeal shall abate. Yea, so many were the Niceties of Appeals, which formerly were in use, not only in Murther, but in all cases of Felony, and so full of Bribery and corruption in the easie composition of all sorts of Murthers and Felonies, and did so much delay the Kings prosecution by Indictment (which was not to begin until the year and day past, after such Felony and murther) in which time commonly the Appellant grew slow in his prosecution, and was many times agreed with, and by the end of the year Witnesses were dead and gone, all was cold and forgotten, as also that the Appellant must sue in proper person, which suit was long and costly, and made the party Appellant weary to sue.

For remedy whereof the Statute of the third of *H.* 7. was made, That *the King shall not* 3 H.7.c.1.

H 4 *stay*

stay until the year and day were past, *but proceed at any time after* **MURTHER.** *the* Murther *committed*; as also, that *the Appellant shall proceed in his Appeal by Attorney*; (all helps the Law could devise to prevent delays in cases of Murther, and to find out and punish the blood-guilty person) observe the penning of that Statute (were there nothing else to be said in this Argument) how necessary it is that all Indictments be made *Murther*, that are brought at the Kings suit within the year and 3 H.7.c.1. day (as the King by this Statute is enabled to do, the words whereof are as followeth, *And if it happen*, *that any person named as principal*, *or accessary*, *he acquitted of any such Murther at the Kings suit within the year and the day*, *that then the said Justices shall not suffer him to go at large*, *but either remit to Gaol*, *or Bail him*, *at discretion*, *until the year and day be past*. And further in the said Statute it is said,

If

If the MURTHERER *escape the Town shall be amerced;* as also, that *the Coroners shall return their Inquisitions before the Justices of Gaol-delivery, and they shall proceed against such* Murtherers; and as it is before in the said Statute, *The King shall not stay until the* year and day *were past, but proceed at any time after the Murther committed:* So that (*prima facie*) the Statute looks upon all Manslayers (unlawfully) to be guilty of *Murther.* And so the Indictment ought to be drawn, or they cannot be continued in Gaol, nor Bailed by this Statute until the year and day be out, nor the Town amerced for such escape, nor the offender proceeded against by the King, within the year and day by Indictment.

Now generally (in these days) since the making of that Statute, all proceedings in Murther and Felony are by Indictment at the Kings suit, not but that the prosecution by Appeal is still in force, and the

the party hath his election which
way he will proceed, either by
Appeal at his own fuit, or by Indictment at the Kings fuit; yea,
even after the Trial had by the
Kings fuit (in fome cafes) although
at the Kings fuit they have been
acquitted of the murther (but
that the abufe of thefe and many
other obfolete Laws) hath taken
away the frequent ufe of them;
except it be through the mifcar-
riage of Grand Jurors, and Jurors
of life and death, in cafes of murther, the one in not fully prefenting the murther, the other in not
confcientioufly giving a Verdict
according to their Evidence, and
thereby provoking the party
(whofe Relation is flain) to the
nice and chargeable remedy of an
Appeal; upon fuch Appeals feveral have been executed after
they have been acquitted by trial
at the Kings fuit upon Indictment, one Woman in my time
in *Berkfhire*, for petty Treafon
for killing her Husband, after fhe
had

had been acquitted for the fame
fact at the Kings fuit by Indictment, was convicted upon the
Appeal, and burnt at a ftake.

Look how high the Appellant
fhall draw his Appeal againft the
Appellee or Defendant, as if for
Murther; in this cafe, if the Appellant fhall furceafe to profecute
fuch Appeal, as by Nonfuit, Re-
leafe, Retraxit, the Woman by
marrying a Husband, *pendente lite*,
or by the Act of God, as if the
Appellant die, or by the Act of
the Law, as if the Appellant take
the priviledge: Now in all the
former Cafes, where the Appeal
ceafeth by the Act of the Appellant (that is, he that profecuteth
the Appeal, after declaration in the
Appeal) the Defendant fhall not
go at liberty, but fhall be Arraigned upon the fame Declaration at
the Kings fuit, for that it doth appear by the Declaration there is a
Murther committed, and the year,
day, and place, when, and where
the fame was committed, and the
                              fame

fame is not tried ; and the Law will not allow fuch great Offences whereof it taketh notice) to be concealed and remain unpunifhed, neither will the King at his fuit fuffer it to be extenuated into a leffer degree of Murther, than the Appellant did : fo careful have the Laws ever been in punifhing of Murther, and revenging Innocent blood, which it feems (and as before is obferved) whilft Appeals were in ufe, and the Kings fuit muft ftay until the year and day were paft, many Murtherers efcaped unpunifhed, and the killing of men was made (as now it is) a trick of Youth, Valour, Hectoring, and Jeft, in regard of fo great impunity it found, by frequent Pardons, Indulgence of Grand Jurors, and others.

And truly, it is much with us in this Age, as it was in thofe daies when Appeals were in ufe, and had the preheminence of the Kings fuit ; Never more killing of men by Duels, Tavern, and

Game-

Game-houfe Quarrels, and yet
never more impunity to fuch Man-
killers, fuch valiant murtherers of
their fellow Chriftians, efpecially
if the Mankiller have either a
fame for Honour or Valour, Mony,
or Intereft of Friends, to procure pity, or pardon and com-
paffion from the Grand Jury., to
find it Manflaughter (if they will
go fo high) where it is Murther,
and then (through that falfe glafs)
to reprefent it to a moft Merciful
King, and thereby obtain a Pardon for the whole offence; or elfe,
upon his Arraignment fhall confefs the Manflaughter, and procure a refpect of his burning in
the hand (becaufe a Gent-hand
killed the man) and afterwards
procure a Pardon for that burning
in the Hand, which the King may
grant, it being no part of the
Judgment, but a notifying the
Perfon, that by that Mark he
may be known again, once to have
had his Clergy, that he may not
have it a fecond time.

Many

Many Recent, and fresh Instances (in particular Cases of blood) might be given (were it safe or seasonable to make reflections) of divers Murthers, that have too easily slipt through the hands of Justice, by the averseness, ignorance, or partiality of Grand Jurors in not observing the direction of the Judges in this particular of finding Bills Murther, instead of Manslaughter, yea, and that many times upon directions given in Court, after open Evidence, which open Evidence to a Grand Jury (especially in Cases of blood) ought to be avoided as much as may be, in regard it doth too much lay open and betray the Kings Evidence, to standers by, it may be Friends of the Prisoner, that may make too much use of it for the benefit of the Prisoner, and prejudice of truth; besides, many Witnesses, although upon their Oath) will not speak so fully in Court before the Bill found, and happily in the presence of

of the Party, or his Friends, as in
a Grand Juries Chamber; more
private befides, where it is before-
hand known, what witnefs-pinch-
ing endeavours will be ufed to
keep him off, or by fome finifter
way to be complied with to leffen
or hinder his Teftimony to the
fecond Jury (if there be occafion)
befides, the Kings Evidence (before Iffue joyned betwixt the King
and the Prifoner) is alwaies to be
fecret, only open to the Grand
Jurors, who are alwaies ftyled,
Juratores pro domino Rege, the
Kings Jury, and are fworn to keep
the Kings Counfel, their Felons,
and their own: now the Witneffes for the King are faid to be
of the Kings Council, which would
abate much of their Oath, if E-
vidence, and the Kings Informations (in Cafes of Bloud) fhould
be open and common.

And as you have heard, what
great Inconveniences were in the
ufe and abufe of Appeals in the
Reign of King *Henry* the Seventh,

so indeed as many (if not more
Inftances of mifchief and inconvenience might be given of Grand
Jurors in this Age (the beft things
corrupted proving the worft) you
may conceive what great complaints have formerly been made
againft Grand Jurors in Parliament in erring upon both hands,
by taking too much liberty to
themfelves, and not obferving the
directions of the Court, that there
was a neceffity of making an Act

3 H. 8.

of Parliament, in the 3 *H.* 8.
(immediately after Appeals began
to fall off) as you may read in
that Act of Parliament made to
reform them, and to reform the
Sheriffs power in retorning them;
the whole Authority of retorning
Inquefts (to take Indictments)
being by force of the Statute of
the 11 *H.* 4. in Sheriffs and Bayliffs of *Franchifes.* It is obferved
by the Statute of the 3 of *H.* 8.
that by reafon of Bribing of Sheriffs, and their Bayliffs and Officers, many true and fubftantial
perfons

perfons were divers times wrongfully indicted of Murther, Felonies, and other Mifdemeanours,
to the utter lofs of their Lives,
Goods, and Lands: And fometimes
alfo great Felonies and Murthers
were concealed, and not prefented by the Grand Jurors, par-
tially retorned by the Sheriffs or
their Minifters; for the preven-
tion whereof, it was eftablifhed
by the faid Act of the 3 *H*. 8.
That *all Pannels of Grand Ju-*
rors, put in by any Sheriff before
any Juftice of Goal-delivery, and
Juftices of Peace, one being of
the Quorum, *in the open Seffions*
to enquire for the King, fhall be
reformed, by putting to, and taking
off the Names of the perfons
which fo be impannelled by every
Sheriff, at the difcretion of the
faid Juftices, before whom fuch
Pannel fhall be retorned, and the
Sheriff upon pain of twenty pound
fhall allow of fuch Pannel, fo re-
formed and retorned by the Jufti-
ces, the one half to the King, the

I   *other*

other to him that will sue for the
same, and the Kings Pardon shall
not be a bar to his part that so
sues. So careful were the Law-
makers to have faithful Jurors,
that should neither accuse the Innocent, nor excuse the Nocent,
and that especially (in Cases of
Blood) should make no concealment.

And lest all this care and re-
formation of Grand Jurors should
do no good, but that they should
still espouse their own opinions,
and make head against the Court,
and wilfully conceal Offences they
were charged to enquire of, there
is a Statute yet in force, 3 *H.* 7.
in which it is ordained, That
the Justices of Peace may (in
their discretions) cause an Inquest
to be Impannelled, to enquire of
the concealments of other Inquests
taken before them, of such mat-
ters and offences as. are to be en-
quired and presented before Ju-
stices of Peace, whereof com-
plaint shall be made. And if any
conceal-

3 H. 7.
of concealment.

*concealment ſhall be found by any
Inqueſt, within one year after
the ſaid concealment, every perſon of the ſaid Inqueſt, that made
ſuch concealment, ſhall be amerced
or fined at the diſcretion of ſuch
Juſtices of Peace, the ſaid A-
merciaments ſo aſſeſſed in plain
Seſſions. And theſe Amerciaments
or Fines may be very high, according to the nature of the Concealment and quality of the perſon.* This Statute only concerns
and remedies Concealments by
Grand Jurors, before Juſtices of
the Peace, at the Seſſions of the
Peace, as conceiving Grand Jurors
would be bolder there, and take
more liberty in their Preſent-
ments than they durſt before Juſtices of Aſſize, Oyer, and Terminer, or Goal-delivery; as alſo,
that ſuch Juſtices and Judges knew
better how to deal with them, if
they made any ſuch concealments
or miſpriſion before them: For
the Grand Jurors being immediate and ſubordinate Miniſters and

Officers

Officers in, and to the Court, and
anſwerable for their Duty there,
as Coroners, Conſtables, and o-
ther Miniſters of the Court, they
may and muſt ſtand to the Judgment of the Court; and in caſe
of any wilful contempt, miſde-
meanor, and concealment, may,
without Indictment, (for how
can they be indicted at the ſame
time by themſelves) be fined by
the Court, as any other Officer
and Miniſter of the Court.

And let Grand Jurors take heed,
leſt by their remiſneſs and pee-
viſhneſs, they give not occaſion
to the making of the like Statute
as was made in the 11. of *H.* 7.
c. 3. upon the ſurmiſe in the Statute, *That whereas many great
Offences, as Riots, unlawful Aſſemblies, Extortions, Mainten-
ances, Imbraceries, and other
Offences, could not be duly puniſhed by the due Order of the Law,
except it were firſt found and preſented by the Verdict of Twelve
men thereto duly ſworn, which
will*

11 H. 7. c. 3.

will not find, nor yet present the Truth (obferve here what occafions Grand Jurors had then given through their neglect) It was therefore provided and enacted by this Statute, *That Juſtices of Aſſize, and Juſtices of Peace, upon Information for the King* (that is meerly upon the Teſtimony of Witneſſes, without Indictment, or uſe of Grand Jurors) *ſhould proceed to make out Proceſs, Puniſh and Condemn Offenders by their Diſcretion, as if it were upon Indictments found by Grand Jurors.* Which Statute was a great Infringment of the Common Law, and the Liberty of the Subject of *England*, who ought not by *Magna Charta*, and the Law of this Land, to be proceeded againſt, or condemned in their Perſons or Eſtates (in Criminals) but by Indictment firſt had and found againſt them by Grand Jurors. It is true, that Treaſons, Murthers, and Felonies, and ſuch Offences (for which life and member ſhould

I 3   be

be loft) are excepted out of this
Act (although they ftand upon the
fame Reafons as the other Offences named in the Act). For by
this Act and new Law, the Subject might lofe his Liberty, fuffer
Ranfom, Stigmatizing, Pillory,
Imprifonment, lofs of Lands and
Eftate (things very near to Life
and Member). And the Lord
Coke tells us, *That* Empfon *and*
Dudley (*two Judges (by reafon
of this Act) committed upon the
Subjects infufferable Oppreffions:*
and therefore this Statute was juft-
ly Repealed after the Deceafe of
H. 7. by the Statute of the 1. of
H. 8. *c.*6. *A good Caveat to Parliaments* (fays the Lord *Coke*) *to
leave all Caufes to be meafured
by the Golden and ftreight Mete-
wand of the Law, and not to the
uncertain and crooked Cord of
Difcretion.* And as good a Caveat it is to Grand Jurors in cafes of Blood, not fo much to be
led by the crooked Cord of Difcretion, as the ftreight Rule of
the

the Law , and Directions of the
learned Judges , who fhould beft
know the Law, and the trueft
meafure thereof : For if the Rule
be true (as indeed it is) *Quod
nihil relictum eft arbitrio Judicis*)
that nothing is left to the Will of
the Judge , much lefs , *arbitrio
Juratorum* , to the will of Grand
Jurors, they having been (through
too much connivance) by an evil
practice , corrupted herein. But
errores ad fua principia referre ,
eft refellere , To bring Errors to
their beginning , is to fee their
laft.

Now, haply Grand Jurors may
conceive , and argue thus ; *That
to extenuate an Offence, is not to
conceal it, if they find it not Murther , yet they find it in fome degree of Manflaughter, &c. Befides, if the Kings Council will
put into the Indictment the words
(Ex malitia præcogitata, &c.)
which only make it Murther, and
which is matter of Fact , they
muft make it out to us , that there*
was

was malice, either from our own knowledge of it, or that it is clearly proved to us from words or deeds expreß, by such an act, that lies in proof, or we are not bound to find those words, but must strike them out of the Indict-ment, or find an Ignoramus: Or if the Witneſſes themſelves shall inform us, that it was a ſudden falling out, or done by misfortune, Se defendendo, in his own de-fence, or to defend himself againſt one that would have robbed him, in his Houſe, or upon the High-way; or that he that did it was a Watchman, a Conſtable, or law-ful Officer, or Keeper of a Park or Warren, and in doing his Du-ty; or that he that did it was a natural Fool, one not Compos men-tis, a Mad-man, or a young Child that did it, and by his young and tender years not capable of malice, and ſo could not be guilty of Mur-ther; or if there had been former fallings out and differences be-twixt them, yet all was reconciled,

ciled, and they good friends a-
gain, and this only a cafual and
fudden difference betwixt them
upon a new occafion, and exceed-
ingly provoked unto it by him that
was flain, fo that we cannot be
fatisfied to find it Murther in any
of thefe cafes, being upon our
Oaths to make true Inquiry, and
if we find not the malice (being
matter of Fact) another Jury can-
not try it. Befides, we have for-
mer practice of our fide, other
Grand Jurors have had, and ta-
ken the fame Liberty, and why
fhould not we? The Judges like-
wife in their Charges inform us
of all the fpecifical differences in
Manflaughter, which we conceive
they intend we fhould take notice
of, as it comes in proof before
us, in our Inquiry. This, I conceive, is as much as Grand Jurors
have faid, or can alledge for themfelves (where they are not pofitively partial, and go clearly a-
gainft their Evidence) why they
do not, or will not (for fuch is
                                 fome

some of their Language) find it
Murther in all Cafes, as the Court
directs, and as the Bill of Indictment is drawn and fent to them as
the King's Declaration.

To fatisfie thefe reafonings and
miftakes (though fufficient hath
been faid already to fatisfie a wife
and fober Grand Jury-man, efpecially in a Cafe of Blood, which
can never receive too ftrict an Inquifition by a Grand Jury, the firft
Inquifitors of it in Court) let them
obferve, that neither themfelves,
nor the party accufed, can be pre-
judiced by what they fhall fo find,
be it never fo high: Firft, not
themfelves; they do but prefent a
probable Accufation (no Conviction) againft fuch a perfon that
hath had his hands in Blood, hath
kill'd a man, is *Vir fanguinis*:
And here certainly it will be the
beft fatisfaction to Confcience (and
that is the beft Friend we can fatisfie) to have all the Circumftances of the Fact (as they are laid
in the Indictment) to be more judicially

dicially and circumspectly examined, sifted, and tryed out, by another Jury, by a Learned Judge, in a publick Court, to the parties face, where the King's Witnesses, and the party himself, and his Witnesses, may be fully heard, and the whole matter fully tryed and debated, which cannot be done in a Grand Juries Chamber, but is altogether stifled and obstructed, if the Grand Jurors suffer it not to come to this Judicial Test and Tryal, but shall put out the words, *Ex malitia præcogitata,* or otherwise alter the King's Declaration and Indictment, which already hath had proceedings in it, and that in Court of Record, where it hath been advised by the Kings Council upon perusal of Informations and Examinations from Justices of Peace or Coroner, in that Case certified to the Court, and upon hearing the Prosecutor and his Witnesses, and so drawn and presented to the Court, Witnesses sworn to it, and Indorsed, *Jurat.*

in Curia, sworn in Court, and
so become something more than
an ordinary Declaration or Writing in Parchment, to be altered
by any, without advice or direction of the Court; for if it might be
so, the King's Council and their
Advice (together with the Judges in such Cafes) would signifie
very little in drawing or advising
any Indictment of Murther, if
Grand Jurors in their Chamber
may (from their own advice) alter it as they please, the Judges
themselves being as well concern'd, in Conscience, to do right
to the Prisoner and Party accused,
as Grand Jurors can be. And also admit that the Witnesses shall
inform the Grand Jury that it was
a passionate and sudden falling out,
or that it was done unawares, or
in his own defence, it is but what
they apprehend it to be; they can
inform but what they saw, or
heard, or believe; they are in the
Affirmative only, and can prove
but for that instant the Fact was
done;

done; they dare not fwear that there had been no falling out before: and as they cannot, or haply will not, prove an exprefs malice, fo neither can they fwear that there was none at all, or not fuch a malice as the Law implies; neither can the Witneffes judge in all Cafes, what is Manflaughter at Common Law, what upon the Statute, what *per Infortunium*, what *fe Defendendo*, what is Juftifiable, or what is Murther: neither indeed in all thefe Cafes, can the Grand Jurors, nor is it convenient for them to judge of all the fpecifical differences, each Circumftance may fo much alter a Cafe; and will they then, by their uncertain Judgments, in cafe of Murther, conclude and preclofe the Court, and determine the Law, that this Fact of Blood fhall go no higher than they pleafe to adjudge it; as in the cafe put of a Child that kills another, not the Grand Jury (who fee not the Child) but the Court, and
the

the other Jury fhall infpect the
Child, fhall judge whether the
Child could do fuch an Act, *fel-
leo animo, ex malitia præcogitata*, and fo be guilty of Malice
and Murther; the Court, and not
the Grand Jury, being to judge,
an malitia fupplebit ætatem, whether upon hearing him fpeak, he
may be thought capable of malice
(as fome at more tender years are
than others) fo in the cafe of a
Fool, or a Lunatick, a Dumb or
Deaf perfon; fo in the cafe of a
Reconcilement after a falling out,
and then a killing; can either Jurors or Witneffes, or any that
hears but one fide, ftate the cafe
aright, or judge whether the Re-
conciliation were perfect or not,
fo as to take away all the feeds of
malice, revenge, or difcontent?
And Mr. Juftice *Stamford* fayes,
*That thofe that are Dumb and
Mute, and Infants, fhall be dif-
charged upon Arraignment.* Which
fhews that they are to be Indicted of Murther : But how fhall they
be

be Arraigned, when they cannot
hear, or speak, and plead ? I conceive by the Inspection and Judgment of the Court upon their Arraignment, I mean, upon the Indictment found by the Grand Jury;
which plainly shews that the
Judges (not the Grand Jurors)
are Judges of the Law, and of
what shall be Murther. So in
the case of killing a Thief that
attempts to Rob or commit Murther, (which is justifiable) this
must judiciously and certainly appear so upon the Tryal, that the
Court may judge whether there
were an intention to Steal, or to
commit Murther, or Rape; and
not let such a Surmise only, *That
there was no such intention*, lead
the Grand Jury to acquit him,
when haply there was such intention. And the Statute of the 24.
of *H.* 8. saith, *That the Party so
Indicted or Appeal'd of such Offence for killing a Thief, or one
that intended to Murther (by
Verdict so found and tryed) shall*

not

*not lose or forfeit Lands or Goods,
but shall be discharged as one
acquit of Felony ; and none can be
acquit of Felony that is not tried
for it* ; the doubt being before this
Statute, Whether he should forfeit his Goods and Chattels as one
that kill'd another by Chance-
medley ? So that there was no
doubt but such a one was Indicted of Murther before this Act, as
one that had kill'd another by
Chance-medly must, and yet is
to be Indicted; Chance-medly
being Manslaughter at Common
Law.

Sure in all these cases, and all
other the like cases of Blood, it is
most prudent and safe for every
wise and conscientious Grand Jury-man (that is satisfied there is
Blood spilt, and the life of a reasonable Creature unjustly taken
away by such a person charged in
the Indictment) rather to presume
it probable, all other Circumstances may be true, as they are laid
in the Indictment (so far as to
make

make an Accusation against a guilty perfon) then that they are not,
and fo to leave it fairly to the
Court to judge thereof, and themfelves free from the imputation of
Blood by concealment; and thereby put the whole matter, with
all its circumftances, upon a moft
legal and impartial Tryal, many
times that appearing upon Tryal that appeared not before.

   And the reafon why a Petit Jury, or Jury of Life and Death,
may extenuate an Offence, and
make it lefs than the Grand Jury,
is becaufe (hearing of both fides)
they may inquire of Circumftances which a Grand Jury cannot. Befides as the (*k*) Lord *Coke*
informs (that Oracle of   (*k*) Coke 3. Inft.fol.26.
the Law) *An Indict-*   1. Inft. Sect. 194.
                         Fortefcue c. 26. 72.
ment is no part of the   Stamford l.2.fol. 90.
Tryal, but an Informa-
tion or Declaration for the King ;
and the Evidence of Witneffes to
a Grand Jury, is no part of the
Tryal: For by Law the Tryal in
that cafe is not by Witneffes, but
            K   *by*

*by the Verdict of Twelve men, and
so a manifest diversity between the
Evidence to a Jury, and a Tryal by a Jury. If the Indictment
were part of the Tryal, then
ought he that is a Noble-man and
Lord of Parliament, to be Indicted by his Peers, for the Tryal
of him ought to be by his Peers;
but the Indictment against a Peer
of the Realm is always found
by Freeholders, and not by
Peers.*

The French word *Enditer* sig-
nifies in Law, an Accusation
found by an Inquest of Twelve, or
more, upon their Oath; and the
Accusation is called *Indictamentum*. And as the Appeal is ever
the Suit of the party, so the Indictment is always the Suit of the
King, and as it were his Declaration, as the Appeal is the Declaration of the party. Some derive
it from the Greek word ἐνδεικνύειν,
to accuse, and as properly may it
be called *Indictamentum ab indi-
dicando, quia aliquid notum facit
dicendo,*

dicendo, he that Accufeth or Appealeth another man, or brings his Crime into queftion, *indiƈta-tus*, *quafi indicatus*; one that hath his caufe fhewed out in publick; (*deferre nomen alicujus, judicare*) to Indiƈt, is to Accufe or Impeach. It fignifies in our Common Law as much as *accufa-tio* in the Civil Law, though it have not the like effeƈt: *Accu-fabilis*, i. e. *accufatione, aut re-prehenfione dignus*, one worthy of Reprehenfion. An Indiƈtment being like the precious Stone of *India*, called *Indica*, which (as *Pliny* notes) in rubbing it break-eth forth into a purple fweat: So doth an Indiƈtment of Murther, which though it feem white and pale in the Grand Jurors hands, afterwards by rubbing and pref-fing hard in Court, breaks out into a purple or bloody fweat (as my felf have very often feen ex-perienced, when Grand Jurors have many times made great fcru-ple even to find the Indiƈtment at

K 2   all)

all) what comes from the Grand Jury is more properly called a Presentment. For the constant form and words in all Bills are, *Jura-
tores pro DominoRege super sacramentum suum præsentant*; observe, they are stiled *Juratores pro Domino Rege* only ; nor can they be otherwise : for they are to hear none but the Kings Evidence, upon his own Declaration : And whoever is to advance (as the Grand Jurors are) but the Interest of one side , ought as rationally to be permitted, to raise and advance it to the highest pitch (that by any reasonable presumption it will bear) as the other side have liberty to extenuate it to the lowest degree and mean that art and cunning (which in these cases of Blood are seldom wanting) can bring it unto ; the one being upon an Accusation against a criminous person, who hath had his hands in Blood , and is certainly guilty in truth of something in the crime he is accused of : The other only

upon

upon his own excuse, who can
never (upon the whole matter)
excuse himself, *à toto*, from the
whole Crime of Blood. If they
are satisfied that it is an Offence a-
gainst the King's Peace, his Crown
and Dignity, and the life of another
person ; it is enough for them to
present the whole matter to the
Court, as the Court hath directed-
ed and advised the Bill to them :
For every Bill of Indictment, that
is formally and legally drawn up,
is presumed to have been seen, advised, and directed (as before is
said) by the Court and the King's
Counsel, upon an Information of
the Fact taken by them
(*l*), (as for the substance
of it, is meet and fit to be
put into such formal and
legal terms for the King)
as it is by the Judges sent
out of Court to the Grand Jurors ;
it being a common practice for the
Judges (according to the matter
of Fact) to direct upon what Statute and Law, and in what manner

(*l*) *The Judges did ad-
vise in drawing the Indictment against* Leak, 4 Jac.
Coke 3. Inst. Tit. Treason,
fol. 16.

K 3

ner and form the Indictment shall
be drawn and sent to the Grand
Jury, that if they find only probable matter contained in it of
accusation in any kind, they may
so present it to the Court, as their
Presentment or Accusation; the
word *Presentment* coming from
the Latin word *Præsentio*, to
smell or scent before, *præsentire
in posterum*, to have a sense of
that which is to come : so if they
have any sense or smell of Blood
in the Indictment, it is enough
for them to leave it to a further
quest of what shall come after:
the Grand Jurors being like the
good Huntsman, that observing
where the Hare hath lately prickt,
or the Deer lately struck, or hath
dropped blood, lays in his Hounds,
and leaves them to make the discovery : so indeed should the
Grand Jurors do the Jury of Life
and Death, in Cases of Blood, and
that the Blood of their fellow
Christians. And thence likewise
the Grand Jurors Presentment is
called

called an *Inquifition*, and themfelves *Inquifitors*, from the Latin
word. *Inquiro, inquirere., quod
vulgo dicitur facere Informatic-
nem*, for every Inquifitor is as an
Informer, a promoter of the Accufation to the Court, in the behalf of the King, that it may
be more judicially enquired into
and determined, which is much
like a Citation of a perfon into
the Ecclefiaftical Courts for a publick fame, which is either fit to
be enquired further into and punifhed, or the party purged or
pronounced Innocent : or like the
Mafters of Requefts to the King
(Honourable perfons) that view
all Petitions and Complaints before they be prefented to the
King, and determine what are fit
to be prefented unto the King, and
what are fit to be rejected.

A ftrong Sufpicion, and the
Fame of the Country may (in
many cafes) be Evidence fufficient
for a Grand Jury to find a Bill;
and here I will leave to the ob-
K 4   fervation

fervation of Grand Jurors, what I
find in Mr. Juftice *Stamfords* Pleas
of the Crown, and which he
himfelf obferveth out of *Bracton*, a very ancient and learned
Lawyer, as *Bracton*'s order in
Cafes of Sufpicion upon
Indictments of Felons(*m*)
de fecta Regum. The
words are thefe, *Nunc
autem dicendum eft de
Indictamentis per famam*
*Patriæ, quum præfumptionem in-
ducunt, & cui ftandum eft donec indictatus fe à tali Sufpicione pur-
gaverit; ex fama quidem oritur
fufpicio, & ex fama & Sufpicione
oritur gravis præfumptio. Tamen
probationem admittit in contrarium five purgationem, Sufpicio
quidem multiplex effe poteft, primo,
fi fama oritur apud bonos & gra-
ves. Item ex facto præcedenti ori-
atur fufpicio cui etiam ftandum eft
donec probetur in contrarium, &c.*
and fo goes on, to let us know the
feveral badges and marks of *Sufpicion*, advifing, that thofe that
will

(*m*) Bracton's *Order in le* ſuſpicion ou Endiĉtments del Felons, *lib.*3. *cap.*22. *paragr.*1. *fol.* 143. Stamf. *fol.*97.

will take Publick fame for an Evidence, take it from those that are of good Fame, and not of evil persons; as he goes on, *Non de malevolis & maledicis, sed providis & fide dignis personis, non semel sed sæpius, quia clamor innuit, & defamatio manifestat; Tumultus enim & clamor populi, quandoque fiunt de multis quæ super veritatem non fundantur. Ideo vanæ voces populi non sunt audiendæ, ut ne dicatur Jesus crucifigitur,* Barabas *autem liberatur.* The whole Chapter is well worth the reading.

And it may not be amiss to observe, that the ancient forms of Indictments or Bills began thus, *Inquiratur pro domino Rege , Let it be enquired of for our Soveraign Lord the King* , as the offence is laid in the Indictment, whether the offence be so (as is there supposed) which is as much as if the Grand Jury should say, *We judge it fit that it be farther enquired of , whether it be truly so*

fo indeed, as it is here fuppofed;
for the Offence, as it is laid in the
Indictment, as it comes from the
Grand Jury (before it receive a
farther trial and enquiry of another Jury) is no more but *Crimen*
fuppofitum & impofitum, an offence
fuppofed and laid to ones charge
to anfwer; and this clearly appears by the Record of every Acquittal or Conviction of any that is
tried upon an Indictment; for the
words of the Acquittal or Conviction (as they are drawn up in
the Record) are thefe, *viz. Ju-*
ratores (that is to fay, the Jury
of Life and Death) *dicunt fuper*
Sacramentum fuum, quod prædi-
ctus A.B. *non eft (vel eft) Culpa-*
bilis de Felonia & Murdro præ-
dict. in Indictamento præd. fpe-
cificat. ei fuperius imponit. modo
& forma prout per Indictamentum
præd. fuperius verfus eum fuppo-
nitur: fo that *fupponitur & im-*
ponitur, fuppofed and impofed,
is all that can be inferr'd from the
Indictment; the Grand Juries
Pre-

Prefentment (upon hearing of
one fide) being the *Suppofition*,
and the other Jury (upon hearing
of both fides) the *Impofition* ; or
Supponitur, and that relates to the
fubftance of the Indictment, as
the Grand Jury fuppofe it to be ;
the *Imponitur*, and that relates to
the *modo & forma* of the Offence,
and the circumftances of it, as it
is laid in the Indictment, as it is
found by the Jury of Life and
Death ; and thefe Circumftances
indeed are the proper enquiry of
the Jury of Life and Death, upon
the hearing of Evidence on both
fides, as appears clearly by the
penning and drawing up of thefe
Records, and all this is no more
than in every common Declaration at the fuit of the Party, only
this Indictment is as a Declaration upon Oath, and muft therefore (for the fatisfaction of thofe
that are fworn) contain, that
which for fubftance feems to them
(*prima facie*) to be a probable
truth, and a tranfgreffion of a
Law,

Law, not strictly looking into the matter and form, aggravations and circumstances of the Fact (as it is laid in the Indictment) for those do but attend and usher in the Fact; but Grand Jurors are principally to eye and look upon the single Fact and act it self, and finding one that hath had his hands in blood, and that probably (upon a farther Enquiry) may become, *reus*, a guilty person, by killing of another person, they are to put their *Billa vera* unto it, although they have no proof at all of the Aggravations and Circumstances that attend the Fact (Evidence many times arising out of the parties own mouth (against himself, upon a strict examination in Court) more than the Witnesses against him have proved.) And it is well observed in theBook called,*The Terms of the Law*,upon these two words,*Billa vera*, where it is said, that *Billa vera* is the Indorsment of the Grand Jury upon any Presentment

or

or Indictment, which they find
to be probably true, (mark thefe
words) *probably true*;nor do I take
the Adjective *Vera* in this place
to fignifie *True*, but *meet*, *reafon*,
or *fit*, and fo it is often ufed in
Terence, and by the Grammarians,
Verum eft, *it is fit*: fo that *Billa
vera* upon the Bill doth not fignifie, a *true Bill*, that hath nothing
but truth in it, but a *meet*, or *fit
Bill* for the further enquiry of
another Jury, which ever fucceeds
fuch an Indorfment of *Billa vera*
by a Grand Jury; certainly it is
upon a great miftake (although I
confefs it is often ufed in Law-
Books, and by wife men) to call
the Prefentment of a Grand Jury
a Verdict, to fay that their In-
dorfing *Billa vera*, or *Ignoramus*
(which is all they do) is their
Verdict, there being a great difference between *Billa vera* and
Veredictum, which fignifies *dictum veritatis*, and even induceth
a Conviction; for nothing can
properly be called a Verdict, but
where

where it is given by a Jury; after
an Iffue joyned, upon hearing of
both fides, *Veredictum*, is, as it
were, *quoddam Evangelium*, like
a little Gofpel of Truth, for indeed every Verdict (which con-
victs a man to the lofs of Life or
Eftate) ought to be as true as the
Gofpel the Jurors fwear upon;
for upon the Iffue of a Verdict, the
Lives and Eftates of all perfons
depend: And therefore an Attaint
lies in Law againft thofe Jurors
that give a falfe Verdict, contrary
to the truth of their Evidence,
which is a Villainous Judgment, a
very great Judgment in Law. And
this Attaint did never by Law, lie,
or was brought againft Grand Jurors for any falfe Prefentment, for
they do but barely prefent an
offence, upon hearing of one fide,
and therefore can be no Verdict
(as from them) the Grand Jury
being for number indefinite, that
being properly called a Verdict
from fuch a Jury, where the Law
makes a determinate number of
twelve,

twelve, or *twenty four*, and no more : Befides, it is alwaies faid in the *Record*, where fuch a Jury finds a Verdict, *Juratores fuper Sacramentum fuum dicunt*, &c. But where the Grand Jury prefent, *Juratores fuper Sacramentum fuum præfentant* (not *dicunt*) there being as much difference between *præfentant* and *dicunt*, as betwixt a known truth, and the report and fame of a fact done.

And this will the better appear, if it be well obferved what Grand Jurors write or Indorfe upon the back of thofe Bills they find; for though they Indorfe fuch Bills (*Billa vera*) yet they never Indorfe upon thofe Bills they do not find (*Billa falfa*) as if one were true, and the other falfe, for fhould they do fo, it would be like an Accufation againft the Profecutor that prefers the Bill, and a great difcouragement to the Kings Evidence ; but they modeftly write (*Ignoramus*) which fignifies to the Court, *they are igno-*
rant

rant *of the matter in the* Bill, *and that they find no cauſe, either from what they have heard from the Witneſſes, or know of their own knowledge, to commend it to a farther Enquiry:* the Verb *Ig-noro,* coming from *Ignarus, not to know, to be ignorant.* And this doth further evince, that the Grand Jurors *Preſentment* cannot proper-ly be called a *Verdict;* becauſe a *Verdict* doth in Law either *convict* or *acquit;* which neither their *Billa vera,* nor *Ignoramus* doth; the firſt is always put to a farther enquiry, the laſt is no acquittal to the party; for although there be many *Igno-ramus's* againſt any perſon, yet may more Bills be preferred a-gainſt the ſame perſon for the ſame offence; for it may be they did not find the Bill, in regard ſome Wit-neſſes were abſent or corrupted, or the matter in the Bill miſtaken; happily it may be no Felony, but ſomething done in jeſt, or in the nature of a Treſpaſs, or a Natural death inſtead of a Murther, or the

Wit-

Witnesses of no Credit, or the like. But if there be any thing of Truth in the Bill proved to them to make a Crime, although not so fully as is laid in the Bill, they muft not in fuch cafe write (*Ignoramus*) as if they knew nothing of a Crime; as if it be a Murther in the Bill, and the Proof reacheth but to an *Infortunium*, or *Je defendendo*, or to any degree of unlawful killing, they muft not write *Ignoramus* upon the Bill; or if Burglary, and the Proof makes it but a fingle Felony, and no Burglary; they muft not Indorfe it (*Ignoramus*) but in all fuch cafes, where they are in any doubt, the beft way for them will be to advife with the Learned Judge, to move the Court for directions therein. It is too great a Scandal to a Grand Jury (Perfons in that quality highly to be efteemed) to fay, that their *Ignoramus* (that is, their *Ignorance*) is

L   their

their Verdict. It is very fafe for Grand Jurors, before they find an *Ignoramus*, to examine every Witnefs produced; but if they have many Witneffes in Murder or Felony, if any one Witnefs induce a ftrong and pregnant Prefumption it is enough, without perplexing themfelves, in haft of bufinefs, they need not examine any more, but put *Billa vera* unto it.

If a Grand Jury find, upon an Indictment of Murther, that *A.* killed *B.* what is it to them (as hath been faid before) whether it be Murther or Manflaughter, whether it were done, *Ex malitia præcogitata, per Infortunium, fe defendendo, in loco & tempore belli,* or otherwife, this is Special matter, and Special matter ought to be found when it is at Iffue by another Jury, and muft arife (I mean the truth of it) *fuper totam materiam* of the Evidence, or proof on both fides; which can never be found and determined by a Grand Jury, that hear but one fide.

side, for very seldom is matter of Fact truly stated in a matter of difficulty, by one side, and therefore (as before is said) the Statute of *Gloucester* provides, that every Man-slaughter, *per Infortunium* or *se defendendo*, shall be found *per Patriam* after the Prisoner hath joyned Issue with the King, and put himself *de bono & malo*, of good or evil, that is, either for his Acquittal or Conviction, *super Patriam;* to be tried by his Country.

And the Jurors of Life and Death themselves are not tied, as not strictly to the form of an Indictment, so not to the whole matter of it; not to the form, as it was well urged by Sergeant *Montague* Reader at the Arraignment of the Earl of *Somerset*, for Murther, by poysoning of Sr. *Thomas Overbury* in the *Tower*, who told the Jury, That *they must not expect visible Proofs in a work of darkness; that many things were laid in an Indictment only for*

form;

form; *that they muſt not look that the proof ſhould follow that*, *but only that which is ſubſtantial*, *and the ſubſtance* (*in that Caſe*) *muſt be this*, *Whether my Lord* of Somerſet *procured*, *or cauſed the poyſoning of Sr.* Thomas Overbury, *or not.* The Lord *Coke* (then Chief Juſtice) and other Judges preſent at the Trial, ſtood up and ſaid, *The Law is clear in this point, that the Proofs muſt follow the Subſtance, not the Form*, *that the Law gives forms in Indict-ments*, *but ſubſtance in proofs.* And yet this was ſpoken to a Jury of Life and Death, who are more carefully to look into Circum-ſtances and Forms (becauſe their error is incurable, if they Convict a man to loſe his life wrongfully) than Grand Jurors are. And I cannot but further obſerve (in this Caſe of Sr. *Thomas Overbury*) that which I would have all Grand Jurors, and Jurors of Life and Death, obſerve, as an Inſtance to guide them in other Caſes of like

like nature, that although it was
laid in the Indictment, That *the
ninth of* May, *Anno* 11 Jac. *Regis,*
Richard Wefton (*who was procured by the Earl of* Somerfet)
*gave to the faid Sr.*Thomas Overbury *a poyfon of green and yellow
colour,called* Rofacre,*in Broth;and
the firft of* June, *Anno* 11 Jac. *Regis* fupradict. *gave him another
poyfon, called* white Arfenick, *and
that the tenth of* June *Anno* 11.
fupradict. *gave to him a poyfon
called* Mercury,*fublimate in Tarts,
and the fourteenth day of* Sep-
tember, *Anno* 11. fupradict. *gave
him a* Glifter *mixt with poyfon
called* Mercury fublimate; (*Ut
pædict.* Thomam Overbury *magis celeriter interficeret,* & *mur-
draret.*) *Et prædictus* Thomas
Overbury *de feparalibus venenis
prædictis,* & *operationibus, inde à
prædictis feparalibus temporibus,
&c. graviter languebat, ufque ad
15. diem* Decembris *Anno* 11. *fupradict. quo die dict.* Thomas *de
prædict. feparalibus venenis obiit*

L 3   *vene-*

venenatus, &c. And albeit it did not appear, or could appear, of which of the said poyfons he died, yet it was Refolved by all the Judges of the Kings Bench, that the Indictment was good; for the fubftance of the Indictment was, *whether he was poyfoned, or not;* and it appeared that *Wefton* within that time aforefaid, had given unto Sr. *Thomas Overbury* divers other poyfons, as namely the powder of *Diamonds*, *Cantharides*, *Lapis Caufticus*, and powder of *Spiders* and *Aquafortis* in a Glyfter. And it was refolved by all the faid Judges, that albeit all the faid poyfons were not contained in the Indictment, yet the Evidence of giving them was fufficient to maintain the Indictment, for the fubftance of the Indictment was (as before is faid) *Whether he were poyfoned, or not.* And when the caufe of the Murther is laid in the Indictment to be *poyfon*, no Evidence can be given of another caufe, becaufe they be diftinct

ſtinɗ and other cauſes : So if the
Murther be laid by one kind of
Weapon, as by a Sword, Dagger,
Stilletto, Stick, Tobacco-pipe,
Knife, Sheers, or other like Wea-
pon, it makes no difference, the
Evidence will be ſufficient, if the
party be ſlain by any of theſe, be-
cauſe they are all under one Claſſis *v.*Mackally's
or cauſe. *Caſe,li.9. ſo.87.*

And afterwards, *Anne Turner*,
Sr. *Gervaſe Elwys*, and *Richard
Francklyn* a Phyſician (Purveyor
of the Poyſons) were Indiɗed as
Acceſſaries before the faɗ done :
And it was Reſolved by all the
ſaid Judges, that either the proofs
of the poyſon contained in the
Indiɗment, or of any other poyſon (although it were out of the
Indiɗment) were ſufficient to
prove them Acceſſaries ; for the
ſubſtance of the Indiɗment a-
gainſt them as Acceſſaries, was,
Whether they did procure Weſton
to poyſon Sr. Thomas Overbury,
or no ? So that it may be obſerved
here, what in the Caſe above was
obſerved

obſerved by the Lo. *Coke* , that *Jurors were not to expect a direct and preciſe Proof in every point laid in the Indictment* ; ſhewing, how impoſſible it were to Convict a Poyſoner, who uſeth not to take any Witneſſes to the compoſing of his ſlibber-ſawces ; neither do other Murtherers , to the contriving of their malice , and manner of killing another , but keep the fire burning in their own boſoms until it break out.

Nor in all Caſes of *Murther* is it material , that expreſs Malice be proved to the Jury of Life and Death, though they be to Convict the Priſoner, much leſs (or not at all) is it material to prove it to the Grand Jury , who are but to preſent it , not to the Jury of Life and death in any caſe where the Law only implies it , for ſuch proof is in the Judgment of the Court and not in the Jury , which the Jury muſt ſubmit unto and be over-ruled in ; much leſs is this implied Malice to be proved to the

Grand

Grand Jury, for it lies not in the proof of Witneſſes, but in the conſtruction of the Law (as is ſaid before;) and yet the Grand Jury muſt find thoſe words, *Ex malitia præcogitata,&c.* as if they were proved expreſly unto them by Witneſſes, or otherwiſe the Jurors of Life and Death cannot enquire of the offence (as (*n*) *Murther :*) And the Jury of Life and Death (in ſuch a Caſe) muſt find thoſe words expreſly, although they cannot be proved unto them, but are only implied and ſupplied by Law, or elſe the party accuſed can never be Convicted of Murther, as might be inſtanced in very many caſes, take ſome for all (*viz.*) One in priſon kills his Keeper, and makes an eſcape, where no malice or falling out can be proved; a ſtranger, or other perſon kills a Watchman, Conſtable,

(*n*) Murther *is a wilful killing of a man upon malice, forethought (but this muſt either be expreſſed in proof, or implied by Law) it ſeemeth to come of the* Saxon *word*, Mordren, *which ſo ſignifieth ; and* Mordridus *is,* the Murtherer, *even to this day amongſt them in* Saxony, *from whence we have moſt of our words: Or it may be derived of* Mort eſt dire, *as* Mors dira, Terms *of the Law,title* Murther, *fol.* 207.

ble, or other Officer, that hath good warrant to ſtay him, though happily there be no cauſe for his ſtay, being an Innocent perſon, or another perſon, and not the ſame they intended; heres no Malice, yet this is Murther *ex malitia præcogitata*, &c. One goes into the Street, or High-way, and kills the firſt man he meets, although he did never ſee him before; The Father or Mother takes their ſucking Child, and daſheth out the Brains of it againſt the wall; Two perſons are fighting a Duel together upon cool blood, upon premeditate malice, and a third perſon comes to part them, and is killed by one of them, this is Murther *ex malitia præcogitata*, in him that killed him (if not in both) although neither of them ever ſaw him before, and yet no malice to this man: (*o*) One wilfully kicks or wounds a Woman

(*o*) *Si ſit aliquis qui mulierem pregnantem percuſſerit ſi puerperium non formatum, vel animatum fuerit & maximè ſi animatum, fecit homicid.* Stamf. *fol.*12. In this fol. you ſhall find Juſtice *Stamford* uſing the words *homicid. & murdrum*, as ſignifying the ſame. v.*Stamf.* fol.21.c.13.

great

great with Child, whereby the
Child is wounded in her, fhe is
afterwards fafely delivered of the
Child(theChild alive)the wound or
bruife by the kick or blow appearing upon theChild mortally,where-
of afterwards it dies,this is Murther
ex malit.præcog. and yet what malice had this man to the Child he
never did fee? Divers perfons are
unlawfully hunting in a Park, one
of them kills the Keeper (after the
Keeper had duly, according to his
Office, admonifhed him to ftand)
all the reft of the Company (although a mile off in the faid Park,
and out of fight) are guilty of
wilful Murther of the Keeper, and
yet nothing of malice can be exprefly proved. One is fhooting at
a Cock or a Hen, and kills another
perfon, this is Murther, his act
was unlawful. One finding a Gun
or Piftol charged, lying upon a
Table, or other place, takes it up
into his hands, draws up the Cock
(not thinking it to be charged) and
in a jefting way gives fire at one in
the

the Room, the Gun goes off and kills him; this is Murther, he had nothing to do to meddle with the Gun, it was out of his Calling, and none of his, he muſt Jeſt at his peril. A Drunken-man gets upon a Horſe (which a ſober perſon might ride quietly) and in a Fair or Market occaſions the Horſe to run over another perſon, and kills him; this is Murther. *A* gives *B* the lie, with many other provoking words, as Coward, Thief, Murtherer, whereupon *B* ſtrikes *A*, and kills him; this is Murther *ex malitia*, &c. words are not a ſufficient provocation for one man to kill another. If one killeth another without any provocation (actual) of the part of him that is ſlain; this is Murther, the Law implieth Malice. If a man knowing that many People are coming along the Street from a Sermon, throw a Stone over a wall or houſe, intending only thereby to fear them, and thereupon one is killed with the Stone; this is Murther, although

Coke li.9. fo.67. 6. in Mackally's Caſe.

3. Inſt.fol.57.

though he knew not the party
flain.   If *A* affault *B* to rob him,
and in refifting *A* killeth *B* ; this
is Murther by malice implied, although he never knew him.

If one meaning to fteal a Deer 3 *Inft. fol. 56.*
in a Park, fhooteth at the Deer,
and by glance of the Arrow killeth a Boy that is hidden in a Bufh ;
this is Murther, the Act being unlawful, though here was no intent
to hurt the Boy, knowing nothing
of his being there.

If a Woman being quick with 22 Ed. 3.
Child, do wilfully with a potion, or *Coron.*263.
otherwife, intend the deftruction
of the Child in her womb, the
Child being born alive, dieth of
the potion, battery, or other caufe;
this is Murther.

If one keep a Maftiff-dog, that
is ufed to bite people, near the
Common Highway, or a Bull or
Beaft, that hath hurt any one (after notice) they kill any one, it
will be Murther in the Owner, although not prefent when the fact
was done; and yet in this, and
                                    the

the other precedent Cafes, he
no exprefs Malice to be proved
what the Law conftrues to be
which can in no fenfe be left to

(p) Murther is (*p*) Grand Jury to be judge
interpretative But in all thefe Cafes, and n
in the Law, and
not to be left to more, muft be ruled and c
Grand Jurors ruled by the Judgment of
opinions. Court, in point of Law.

      Although no Malice in t
Cafes can be proved to the G
           Jury or petit Jury,
(q) Aliquando vero clan- yet the Indictment
culum & nemine vidente,
ita ut sciri non possit quid be exprefly drawn, ar
sit actum, hujusmodi homi- found by the Grand J
cidium dici poterit Mur-
drum. Stamf.6. 1.fol.12. with thefe words to n
Hales & Petty Cafe *in his* it Murther, *Ex ma*
Comment. *sua præcogitata,&c.*

      is, that he killed hir
of his malice, fore-thought;
that thefe words make a nev
fence of Felony and Murther,
was not Felony and Murther
fore, and fo efteemed in all C
where it was done voluntarily
by affault; and this appears pl
ly by the Statute of *Marlebr*
(formerly mentioned) 35 F

where it is faid, *Murther from henceforth fhall not be adjudged, before our Juftices, where it is found by Misfortune only, but it fhall take place in fuch as are flain by Felony, and not otherwife.* By this Statute it is plain, that killing one unawares, by misfortune, was Murther before this Statute, and that after this Statute, all other killing, where it is Felony, fhall be Murther, as before this Statute, *Felony* is a general term, which comprehendeth divers hainous offences, for which the Offender ought to fuffer death, and lofe their Goods and Lands. They are called *Felonies* of the Latin word *Fel*, which is in Englifh *Gall*, in French *Feil*, or of the ancient Englifh word *Fell* or *Fierce*, or becaufe they are intended to be done with a cruel, bitter, fell, fierce or mifchievous mind.

Terms of the Law, Felony 160. fol.

So the Statute *de Officio Coronatoris*, made 4 *Ed.* 1. (where the Coroner is well directed his duty) where any perfon is flain, or fuddenly

4 Ed. 1.

denly dead, how he fhould behave himfelf, which is worth his reading. It follows in the faid Act in thefe words, *And if any be found Culpable of the Murther, the Coroner fhall immediately go to his houfe, and Inventory his Goods, Chattels, Lands, &c.* (as in that Act is further directed) I only mention it to fhew, that all that were found fo flain, the Coroner was to enquire of it, as Murther, or otherwife there could be noInventorying ofGoods, valuing, or feizing of Lands, &c. or committing the Offender to the Goal by the Coroner, as plainly doth appear by that Act.

2 Ed.6.c.24.   So the Statute of the fecond of *Ed.* 6. where one is ftricken in one County, and dies in another (it being doubtful before where the Trial fhould be) gives power to the party concerned, to bring an Appeal (who had not power to Appeal in that cafe before) of Murther only in the County where the party dies, and in that cafe

cafe can bring no Appeal of Manflaughter (as in the ftreightned
fenfe fome would take the word
Manflaughter) by this Statute is
declared, That *where any* Murther
or *Felony*(which word *Felony* here
cannot comprehend *Manflaughter*) *fhall be committed in one
County, and there be Acceffaries
to the fame in another County;
upon an Indictment found in the
County where fuch Acceffaries are
guilty, the Certificate of the Conviction or attainder of the Principal fhall be good, to proceed a-
gainft fuch Acceffaries :* So that if
the Principal be not Indicted of
Murther, I conceive it is doubtful
upon this Statute, to proceed to
the Condemnation and Judgment
of the Acceffary in another County, for by no congruity can the
words *or Felony* comprehend
Manflaughter. A Pardon of all
Felonies will hardly pardon Manflaughter, or be allowed of.

M So

4 H. 7. c. 13.

So in the 4th of *H. 7. cap.* 13. there are thefe words in the Sta-tute, *Whereas upon truſt of the priviledge of the Church, divers perſons have been the more bold to commit Murther, &c. becauſe they have been continually admit-ted to the benefit of the Clergy as oft as they offended; It is enacted, That every one being once ad-mitted to have the benefit of his* (r) *Clergy (if not within Holy Orders) ſhall not a ſecond time be admitted for ſuch an offence. And that every perſon ſo Convicted for Murther, to be marked with an* M *upon the brawn of the left Thumb, and for another Felony with a* T.

(r) *When Clergy began appears not by any Common Law book, it takes its root from a Conſtitution of the Pope, that the Prieſts ſhould not be accuſed before a Secular Judge.*

Co. Magna Charta 636. *It hath been confirmed by divers Parliaments, and ſo favourably uſed by the temporal Judges, that it hath been al-lowed to all Lay-men that could read, which is more than the Com-mon Law requires.* Stamford fol. 123. *The firſt that mentions this Priviledge at Common Law is* Bracton, *that wrote in the time of King* Henry *the Third.* Bracton *lib. 3. fol.* 123. *The next is the Statute of* Weſtm. *3 Ed. 1. c. 2. By the* Popes Conſtitutions *the Priviledge of* Clergy *extended to all Offences whatſoever; and the Prelates of* England, *by Colour thereof, did claim the ſame as generally.* vide *9 Ed. 2. Articuli Cleri. Yet within this Kingdom Clergy was al-lowed only in Caſes of* Murther, petty Treaſon, *and* Felony, *not in Treaſon againſt the King himſelf.*

Here

Here it is plain that the word
Murther comprehended all manner of Manſlaughter, all manner
of Felonious killing, every Murther being Manſlaughter, and e-
very Manſlaughter then as Murther, they being *Termini conver-*
tibiles, equally ſignifying the Genus of Man-killing, you may per-
ceive by what hath been ſaid before, that *Felony* cannot comprehend *Manſlaughter* or *Murther*,
for here the one is to be burnt with
an *M* for Murther, the Felon with
a *T* for Theft, both which marks,
upon the reſpective Convictions,
are (as I conceive in thoſe Caſes)
by vertue of this Statute, obſerved
to this day, although we now apply the Letter *M* to ſuch, as the
Jury of Life and Death, upon
an Indictment of Murther from
the Grand Jury, ſhall Convict of
Manſlaughter, that is, upon the
point ſhall find this Special matter, that is to ſay, that there was
no Malice, expreſſe or implied, in
him that killed the other; but in

M 2

a ſudden heat of blood, occaſioned
by an actual (not verbal) provocation in him that was killed.
This contradiſtinction betwixt the
two words, *Murther* and *Manſlaughter* (as I conceive) came
into our Laws only ſince the Statute of the 23 *H.8. c.*1. that takes
away Clergy, that is, will not ac-
cept of them to be Clerks that kill
another maliciouſly. I find not
this diſtinction before, either in
the *Levitical* Laws (the Laws of
God)or the Laws of *England* : No
Sanctuary or place of Refuge (as
is ſaid before) by the Law of God,
being allowed for ſuch a diſtinction, but both ſhould have been
pluck't from the Horns of the Altar; and by our Law, in both caſes
(notwithſtanding this Novel diſtinction) they were equally admitted to Clergies, I mean by the
Common Law.

The ſaid Statute of the 4 *H.* 7.
c. 13. being the firſt Statute (that
I find) that appoints burning in
the Hand for Murther and Felony,
and

and takes away Clergy for the Second offence of the fame kind, where Clergy hath been allowed before ; and it is obfervable , that in this Statute it is called *Murther*, with, or without the words *Ex malitia præcogitata* , not having refpect to our Modern diftinction, which holds only (as is faid) in the enquiry of the Jury of Life and Death , who have the whole matter of Fact before them, with all the circumftances thereof as it arifeth from both fides, which the Grand Jurors neither have , nor ought to have.

Then comes the Statute of the 23 H.8. c.1. 23 *H.* 8. (formerly mentioned) being the firft Statute that takes away *Clergy* for the firft offence of Murther , called in this Statute *Wilful Murther* (s) , of *Malice prepenfed*; this Statute being made to rectifie the great abufe in Ordinaries , in fuffering notorious *Thieves* and *Murtherers* to make purgation ,

(s) *That is, voluntary and of fet purpofe, though it be done upon a fudden occafi- on ; for if it be voluntary, the Law implieth* Malice. Coke 3. *Inft. fol.62.*

M 3 and

and provides, That *no person which hereafter shall be found guilty (after the Laws of this Land) of any petit Treason, or for any Wilful Murther of Malice prepensed, Robbing of Churches, Robbing of Persons in their houses, or upon the High-way, wilful burning of Houses, or Barns with Corn, or Accessaries before the same, shall be from henceforth admitted to the benefit of their Clergy, but suffer death as if they had been no Clerks;* it seems all that were, that is, as many as the Ordinary then esteemed so, *Clerks*, although they were guilty of *Murther*, *petty Treason*, and *Felony*, suffered not death, (so great favour and immunity had they in those times for such bloody and crying sins) so prevalent were the Clergy, and those within Holy Orders, in those daies, that this very Act of Parliament, that takes away Clergy from others, that commit *Murther*, *Burglary*, and *Robbery*, and other Offences before-named, excepts

cepts all within Holy Orders (*t*),
from the fame pains and
dangers other perfons
mult fuffer for the fame
Offences; which freedom
and Indulgence continu-
ed to them in Holy Or-
ders (as they call it) until the
28 *H.*8.*c.*1. which provides, That
they within Holy Orders, *as to*
fuch and other Offences,
(*u*) *fhall be under the*
fame pains and dangers
that others be. Now this
Statute makes none of
the former offences Felony or
Murther, that was not fo before
the making of this Statute, but
only takes from them (that commit any of thefe offences) the
benefit of their Clergy; certainly
there wanted not thofe that committed wilful Murther of Malice
prepenfed (as we now diftinguifh
it) before the making of this Statute; as thofe that committed Sacriledge, robbed perfons in their
Houfes, and upon the High-way,

(*t*) *within five years of the time of King Henry the Second, there were above a* 100 *Murthers by Priefts and men within Holy Orders.*

(*u*) *The Exemption of the Clergy taken away by the Laws of* Clarendon, Graft. 1187.

M 4   wilfully

wilfully fired Houſes, and Barns
with Corn, and were Abettors to
the ſaid Offences: ſo it is very
plain, that this Statute makes no
alteration as to the drawing and
penning of Indictments of *Murther, Sacriledge, Robbery, Burglary, &c.* but only takes away
Clergy from every perſon, who
after the making of that Statute
ſhould be found guilty (as the
words of the Act are, *after the
Laws of this Land*)for any of the
aforeſaid Offences. So that according as the Indictment of Murther was, by the Laws of this
Land, before the making of this
Act, ſo muſt it be after the making
of this Act wilful Murther, in the
Statute 32 *H.*8.*c.* 12. and this Statute of the 23. of the ſame King,
comprehends as well that which
we call *Manſlaughter*, and every
killing where the will of man is
freely engaged, as it doth wilful
Murther of Malice prepenſed;
compare them together, in the
one you will find Clergy taken
... ..
away

away for wilful Murther of malice prepenfed,and Sanctuary from
wilful Murther, and generally
fuch Offences as were prohibited
Sanctuary by former Statutes are
now prohibited Clergy by later
Statutes. The words *Ex malitia
præcogitata*, & *murdravit* (which
now make all this conteft) before
the making of this Statute in a-
ny cafe of Murther, neither ag-
gravated nor extenuated the Offence, made it neither more nor
lefs penal. But fince the making
of this Act, thofe words are made
neceffary in all Indictments and
Convictions of Murther, and principally and only (in cafes of wilful
Murther) to be confidered and
weighed by the Court and Jury of
Life and Death, upon hearing and
debating the matter, with all its
circumftances (as hath been faid
before) on both fides; thofe words
being matter of Law, mixt with
matter of Fact, and are not to be
expunged by a Grand Jury, becaufe
they cannot afterwards be fupplyed

ed nor implyed by the Court, and Jury of Life and Death after the Arraignment of the Prifoner, fhould there appear upon Tryal never fo great caufe, yet *Felonicè* and fome other words (though material) may be fupplyed in a Special Verdict. If upon an Indictment of Murther, *quod Felonicè percuffit, &c.* the Jury find *percuffit tantum*, yet the Verdict is good; for the Judges of the Court are to refolve upon the fpecial matter, whether it was *Felonicè, &c.* or not ?

Cok.lib.9.69.   *Coke lib. 9. 69.* And if the Court adjudge it Murther, then the Jurors, in the conclufion of their Verdict, find him guilty of the Murther contained in the Indictment, and to fhew the power of a Jury of Life and Death (who indeed fhould have the fulleft and higheftCharge can be laid againft the prifoner, for the Offence he is to be tryed). If *A.* be Appealed or Indicted of Murther, *viz.* that he of malice prepenfed kill'd *B.* *A* pleads that

, he

he is not guilty *modo & forma*, yet
the Jury may find *A* guilty of Manflaughter, without malice prepenfed; becaufe the killing of *A.* is
the matter, and malice prepenfed is
but a circumftance, *Plow.Com.* 101. Plow.Com. 101
And generally where *modo & for-
ma*, are not of the fubftance of the
Iffue, but words of form there, it
fufficeth, although the Verdict
doth not find the precife Iffue,
22 *H.8.c.19.*   22 H.8. c.19.

The firft Statute that I find
thefe words mentioned in of ma-
lice prepenfed, is the 22 *H. 8. c.*   22 H.8. c.14.
14. where it is faid, *If any perfon,
for any petty Treafon, Murther, or
Felony, have obtained the King's
Pardon, or is otherwife difcharg-
ed out of Sanctuary, and afterwards commit another petty Treafon, Felony, or Manflaughter by
Chance-medly (and not Murther
of malice prepenfed) and afterwards take Sanctuary again for
any fuch petty Treafon, Felony, or
Manflaughter by Chance-medly, the
fame perfon fhall enjoy a fecond*
                                      pri-

priviledge of Sanctuary: So that
he that committed Murther of malice prepenfed, could not enjoy
the benefit of Sanctuary a fecond
time.

Then comes the Statute of the
25 *H.* 8. *c.* 3. and remedies divers
defects that were in the faid Statute of the 23 *H.* 8. Forafmuch as
the faid Act extended only to fuch
perfons as were found guilty, after the due courfe of the Laws of
this Land, divers and great Rob-
bers, Murtherers, Burglars, and
Felons, did commit thofe Offences,
perceiving, and clearly underftanding (by the words of the faid Statute) that they fhould not lofe the
benefit of Clergy, unlefs they be
found guilty, after the due courfe
of the Law, upon their Arraignment of, and upon the faid Murthers and Felonies fo by them done
and committed, by reafon whereof divers of the faid perfons, upon
their Arraignment of the faid Offences and Felonies upon their Indictments againft them, would
ftand

ftand mute, and fometimes challenge peremptorily over the number of Twenty, or elfe would not
anfwer directly to the fame Indictments whereupon they were
Arraigned according to Law; It
was therefore provided by this
Statute, *That every perfon that*
hereafter fhould be Indicted of
petty Treafon, wilful burning of
Houfes, Murther, Robbery, or
Burglary, or other Felony, ac-
cording to the tenour or meaning
of the faid Statute of the 23 H. 8.
and thereupon Arraigned, and do
ftand mute of malice, or froward
mind, or challenge peremptorily a-
bove the number of Twenty, or
elfe will not, or do not anfwer
directly to the fame Indictment
and Felony whereupon he is fo
Arraigned, fhall lofe the benefit
of Clergy, in like manner and
form as if he had directly plead-
ed to the fame petty Treafon, Mur-
ther, Robbery, or other Felony
whereupon he is fo Arraigned,
(not guilty) and thereupon had
been

been found guilty after the Laws of the Land. Upon the penning of this Act it feems clear that all Indictments for the unlawful or wilful killing of any perfon, ought to be made Murther as they were formerly before this Act. For if the Prifoner fhould be Arraigned upon an Indictment only of Manflaughter (according to the now diftinction of Man-flaughter) and upon his Arraign-ment fhould ftand mute, not An-fwer directly, or challenge per-emptorily, whereby he could have no Tryal, it would be a great queftion, Whether he could have Judgment upon this Act? The words are, *petty Treafon, wilful burning of Houfes, Murther, Rob-bery, Burglary, or other Felonies*; For as it is not named here by the term Manflaughter, fo it can-not (with any congruity) be com-prehended under any of thofe Heads: Not under the general Head of *other Felonies*, after the commemoration of fo many feveral Felonies

Felonies next before, as *Burning of Houses*, *Robbery*, *Burglary*, *and other Felonies*, muft needs be intended of fuch like Felonies or Thefts. And what Judge (in cafe of Life and Death) will proceed upon fuch a *moot point* (or rather a clear Cafe to the contrary) to give Judgment and Sentence of Death upon any by this Act of Parliament.

Then comes the Statute made in the 28 *H.*8.*c.*1.and rehearfeth all thefe former Statutes, *viz.* 22 *H.* 8. 23 *H.* 8. and the 25 *H.* 8. and continues them all until the next Parliament; and provides further, *That fuch as be within Holy Orders, fhall be under the fame pains and dangers that others be;* (all within Holy Orders being by the 23 *H.* 8. excepted in Cafes of Murther, petty Treafon, and Felony, from the pains and dangers that Lay perfons fuffered for fuch offences). It feems thofe in Holy Orders then began to lofe their efteem, as appears more fully

28 H. 8.c.1.

fully in the enfuing Act, which perpetuates the former Acts.

32 H.8.c.3. Then comes the Statute made in 32 *H.* 8.*c.*3. and rehearfeth the fame Acts again, and makes them perpetual ; and Enacts , *That all perfons within Holy Orders, which by the Laws of this Realm ought, or may have their Clergy for any Felonies, and fhall be admitted to the fame, fhall be burnt in the hand, in like manner as Lay Clerks in fuch Cafes, and fhall fuffer all fuch pains, dangers, and forfeitures as Lay perfons in like Cafes.*

1 Ed.6.c.12. Then comes the Statute of the 1 *Ed.* 6. and after it hath declared what Acts fhall be Treafon; declares what Offences fhall be outed of Clergy , *viz. Such perfons, as in due form of the Laws, fhall be attainted or convicted of Murther of malice prepenfed, of poyfoning of malice prepenfed, of breaking of any Houfe by day or by night (any perfon being put in fear) robbing any perfon in or*

near

*near the High-way, felonious
ftealing of Horfes, Geldings, or
Mares, or for felonious taking
of any Goods out of any Parifh
Church, or other Church or Chappel; all Offenders in any of thefe
Cafes fhall be excluded of the benefit of Clergy, whether they be
convicted by Verdict, Confeffion,
or ftand Mute, &c. and that in
all other Cafes of Felony, Clergy
may be allowed.* Here is no mention of petty Treafon, burning of
Houfes and Barns with Corn, and
Acceffaries before, to be outed of
Clergy, as is in the 23 *H. 8. c. 1.*
So that it feems after the making
of this Act, they might have had
their Clergy; the new Offences
added to this Act to be outed of
Clergy (that were not in that
Act of 23 *H. 8.* are only *ftealing
of Horfes, Geldings, and Mares:*
And by this Act *Poyfoning* is made
Murther, although no malice be
proved, and Clergy taken a-
way.

*Poyfoning mur-
ther, although
no malice be
proved.*

N   Then

2 Ed.6. c.24. Then comes the Statute of 2 *Ed.* 6. and this Statute gives remedy in feveral Cafes of Murther and Felony (where there was none before at Common Law). As firft, where one is felonioufly ftricken in one County, and dies thereof in another. Secondly, where one is Acceffary in one County to a Murther, or Felony in another County; before this Statute, no fufficient Indictment in any of thefe Cafes, could be taken in either of the faid Counties; for that by the cuftome of the Realm, the Jurors of the County where fuch party died of fuch ftroke, would take no knowledge of the faid ftroke (being matter of Fact) in a forreign County, although the faid Counties and Places adjoyned very near together; nor the Jurors of the County where the ftroke was given, could take knowledge of the death in another County, although fuch death moft apparently came of fuch ftroke; fo that

such

such Offence (and the other Offences before mentioned) for the like reason remained unpunished; and such Murther could not be proceeded againſt, either by way of Indictment or Appeal: Now this Statute provides, *That an Indictment found by the Jurors of the County where the death ſhall happen, whether it be found before the Coroner, upon ſight of the dead Body, or other Juſtices that ſhall have power to inquire of ſuch Offences, ſhall be as good and effectual in Law, as if the ſtroke and poyſoning had been committed and done in the ſame County where the party ſhall dye, or where ſuch Indictment ſhall be found.*

And likewiſe provides, *That ſuch Party, to whom Appeal of Murther ſhall be given by the Law, may commence, take, and ſue Appeal of Murther, in the ſame County, where the ſame perſon ſo feloniouſly ſtricken or poyſoned ſhall dye, as well againſt the*

Prin-

*Principals, as against every Ac-
cessary to the same Offences, in
whatsoever County or Place the
Accessary or Accessaries shall be
guilty of the same.* And doth further provide, *That where any
Murther or Felony shall be done
in one County, and another person, or more, shall be Accessary, or
Accessaries, in any manner of wise
to any such Murther or Felony
in any other County, that then an
Indictment found or taken against
such Accessary, or Accessaries (upon the Circumstances of such matter before the Justices, &c.) where
such Offence of Accessary shall be
committed, shall be as good in
Law, as if the principal Offence*
Cok.I.9.f.117. *had been committed in the same
County where the same Indictment
against such Accessary shall be
found.*

Here it may be observed, That
the Appeal given by this Statute
to the party, where one is wounded or poysoned in one County, and
dies thereof in another, must be

᷍   an

an Appeal of Murther, otherwife
it will not lye either againft Principal or Acceffary by the words
of this Statute. So in cafe of an
Indictment (where it is faid in
this Statute, *where any Murther
or Felony fhall be committed in
one County, and the Acceffary be
in another County*) here the word
Murther muft be one *Species*, and
Felony, that is Theft, another;
viz. carrying of ftoln Goods into
another County : So that the Indictment in this cafe againft the
Principal muft be Murther, or the
Acceffary thereto is not tryable
in another County ; and there muft
be a Certificate of fuch Conviction or Attainder of the Principal
under the Seals of the Juftices before whom fuch Principal was
Convicted or Attainted, before
fuch Acceffary can be tryed; and
that fhall be fufficient to enable
the Juftices to try the Acceffary in
Murther or Felony in another
County. And although the word
Manflaughter be mentioned in this
N 3   Statute

Statute (as thus, *within the year and day after such Murther and Manslaughter committed*) it is not here mentioned, as any *Species* of Murther, but only as the *Genus* called in this place only Murther and Manslaughter.

5 Ed.6. c.9.   Then comes the Statute of the 5 *Ed.6.* and Resolves three several Doubts or Questions moved upon the Statute of the 23 *H.8.*

This is not much pertinent to this purpose, but that it takes away Clergy, and relates to several Statutes before mentioned concerning murther. *c.1.* The first Doubt was, *Whether Clergy were taken away by that Statute, unleß the very Felony and Robbery were committed in the very Chamber or Place where the Owner, Dweller, his Children, or Servants should happen to be (although they were in some other part of the House).* The second Doubt was, *If it were done in the Chamber, and the parties there asleep, and so not put in fear.* The third Doubt was, *Where such Robberies or Felonies are committed in a Booth or Tent in any Fair or Market, the Owner, Children, or Servants being*

*being then put in fear, whether
Clergy should be taken away by
that Statute in any of these Cases.*

For the clearing of these three
Doubts it was Enacted, *That if a-
ny person be convicted for robbing
any in any part of their dwelling
House, or dwelling Places (the
Owner, his Children, or Servants
being in any part of the said House
or Precincts thereof) whether
sleeping or waking, such Offender
shall not be admitted to his Clergy.   And so he that robs any Tent
or Booth, in Fair or Market,
whether the Owner, his Wife,
Children, or Servants be sleeping
or waking in the same, shall lose
his Clergy.*

Then comes the Statute made $_5$ Ed.6.
in the 5. of *Ed.6.* and takes away
Clergy from those, *That commit
Burglary or Robbery in one County, and carry the Goods into a-
nother County, and are there legally convicted.*

This Statute likewise declares

N 4   This

25 H. 8. c. 3. the Statute made the 25 *H*. 8.*c*.3. shall stand in force, notwithstanding a Clause comprised in the Sta-
1 Ed. 6. c. 12. tute of the 1 *Ed*. 6. *c*. 12. which makes void a Clause in the said Statute, and takes away the force of it in taking away Clergy from such as commit Robberies and Burglaries in one County, and are convicted of the Felony for bringing the stoln Goods into another County. For whereas the said Statute of the 1 *Ed*. 6. *c*. 12. declares, *That such as are convicted or attainted of Murther of malice prepensed, or of poysoning of malice prepensed, or of breaking any Houses by day or by night, (any person there being put in fear) or robbing any person in or near the High-way, or for stealing Horses, Geldings, or Mares, or Felonious taking any Goods out of any Parish Church, or other Church or Chappel, should not have the benefit of Clergy. And that in all other Cases of Felony (other than such as before are*

men-

mentioned) *Clergy should be al-*
lowed in like manner as it might
have been before the 29 *day of*
April, in the first year of King
Henry *the Eighth, by reason of*
which Article or Clause the said
Statute, made in the 25 H. 8.
which did put such Felons and
Burglarors from their Clergy,
that do such Offence in one Coun-
ty, and after are taken with the
Goods stoln in another County,
and there Arraigned and found
Guilty, was made void, to the
great boldning and comfort of such
Offenders: It is by this Act En-
acted, That the said Act made in
the said 25*th year, touching the*
putting of such Offenders from
their Clergy, and every Article, Cok·l.11. f.31·
Clause, and Sentence contained in
the same touching Clergy, shall
from thenceforth (touching such
Offences) stand and be in force.

Then the Statute of 2 & 3 of *P.* Stat.2 & 3 P.
& *M. c.* 17. takes away the benefit & M. c. 17.
of Clergy only from *Bennet Smith,*
for being Accessary to the Murther
of

of *Giles Rufford* before the Murther committed, and for procuring of the fame.

Stat. 4 & 5 P. & M. c. 4. Afterwards the Statute of the 4 & 5 of *P. & M. c.* 4. takes away Clergy from every perfon, *That fhall malicioufly command, hire, or counfel any perfon or perfons to commit any petty Treafon, wilful Murther, Robbery in any* Dier f.18 3,186. Cok.l.11.f.35. *dwelling Houfe or Houfes, Robbery in or near the High-way, or wilfully to burn any dwelling Houfe, or any part thereof, or any Barn having Corn or Grain in the fame.*

Here I had thought to have proceeded, and to have mentioned (in order of time) all fuch Statutes as were made in any King's Reign, to take away Clergy in any Cafe of Felony, but that would be too much to affume another Subject, than what principally is here intended, having made too great a digreffion already, yet not altogether unufeful herein.

Then

Then the Statute made 1 *Jac.*
c. 8. takes away Clergy from him
*that fhall ftab another, that hath
not firft ftricken, nor hath a weapon drawn (if he dye thereof in
fix months, although no malice
can be proved)* except it be done
fe Defendendo, or *by misfortune,
in keeping the peace, or correcting
his Servant or Child.* This with-
.out all queftion was Murther (by
malice implyed) before the making of this Statute ; and fuch a
kind of killing is adjudged Murther
at this day, that is, where one
fhall wilfully kill another (by a-
ny weapon) without provocation
from him in deeds; for no provocation in words [only] will make it
Manflaughter, or lefs than Murther. And (in my judgment) it
is an Error in practice of this Indictment upon the Statute of
Stabbing, to leave out the words
(*ex malitia præcogitata*) in the
Indictment : For the words of the
Statute are (*although no malice
can be proved*) then fure the
meaning

meaning of the Statute is (as in
other cafes) it fhall be implyed:
And in all Indictments, where
malice is only implyed, and cannot exprefly be proved, thofe
words *ex malitia,&c.* muft be put
into the Indictment, to make it
Murther, and to take away Clergy,
and by fuch words the Indictment
will be good, both upon the Statute, and at Common Law.

And fo are the Indictments
made againft lewd Women that
kill their baftard children, upon
21 Jac. c.27.　the 21 *Jac. cap. 27.* although the
fpecial matter of the Statute be
put into the Indictment, *viz.*
*That it is a baftard Child, and
born of her body alive,* yet the
words, *ex malitia præcogitata*,
are always put into the Indictment; which malice the Law implies, although none can prove
the child born alive, and none
can be prefumed to bear malice
to a dead child: And haply it
might be born dead, or dye after
it was born, againft the will of the
Mother,

Mother, of her Throwes and Strivings, to be delivered without help. It is not the burying of the Child, or hiding of it, that makes it Murther upon the Statute (as fome have conceived) for if the Child be found dead in Bed by her fide, or in her bofome, yet it is Murther; for the word [*conceal*] in the Statute, relates not to the Body of the Infant, but the death of it; the words being thefe, *Shall fo conceal the death thereof, that it may not come to light* (that is, to the knowledge of one Witnefs at leaft) *whether it were born alive or not, but be concealed, fhe fhall fuffer death as in cafe of Murther:* If fhe can prove by one Witnefs it was born dead, then her hiding or burying it afterwards will not be Evidence againft her to take away her Life upon that Statute.

Thefe two Statutes create no new Offence that was not Felony and Murther before, but only take away Clergy in thofe two cafes, the

1 Jac. c. 8.
21 Jac. c. 27.

the one of fudden and defperate
ftabbing (then frequently in ufe)
the other of lewd Whores, who
having committed one fin, to a-
void their fhame, and the charge
of a Baftard, would commit a
greater, by trufting to their own
ftrength in their Delivery, that
they might more privately deftroy the Infant, and yet avoid
the danger of the Law, becaufe
in that cafe, none for the King
could prove the Child born alive,
and therefore it was impoffible to
Indict and Convict her at the common Law for Murther, although
really and in truth it were fo. This
Statute makes theSuppofition good
for the King to the Grand Jury,
and Jury of Life and Death, and
to the Judgment of the Judge in
point of Law, that the Child
(x) *Note this* (fuppofed to be murthered) was
the Grand born (x) *alive*, and by her
find as it
in the
by the Kings Counfel, that the Child was born alive,
though they have not the leaft Evidence for it, and yet I truft they
are not forfworn.

mur-

murthered, in regard fhe being a lewd woman, and contrary to the Cuftome of honeft and innocent women (who always defire help in their Labour) chufeth to be delivered alone, this Statute puts the proof upon her (if fhe will avoid fo ftrong a prefumption of Murther) to be fure to have one Witnefs to prove the Child was born dead. It being likewife ftrongly prefumed, that a woman (without help of fome other) cannot be delivered of a Child at full growth dead in the Womb.

Two remarkable Cafes I have known in my time upon the faid Statute of 1 *Jac.* in *Oxfordfhire* Circuit; the one in Mr. Juftice *Jones* his time (a Learned Judge that went Sixteen years together that Circuit) where the Cafe was; A cunning defperate Fellow, having an intention to ftab another perfon, and yet to avoid coming within the danger of that Statute, had (to that purpofe) provided himfelf of a Dagger naked in his
Pocket

Pocket (he being never known to
wear any before) came into an
Alehouſe where the party was he
intended to ſtab, and at firſt coming uſed very friendly Language
unto him, but afterwards all the
provoking Language he could,
to make the other ſtrike him;
which the other no ſooner held
up his ſtick to have done, but he
ſtabb'd him into the Body with
his Dagger, whereof he dyed:
No malice could be proved, yet ſo
much of his intention by his pre-
paration and circumſtances appearing to deſign the ſtabbing of
the other, that it was adjudged to
be within the meaning, though
not within the Letter of the
Statute, the Lord Chief Baron
Davenport being the other Judge
of that Circuit) and he was deny-
ed his Clergy, and after Judgment
was Executed. It being then obſerved by the Judges, That immediately after the making of that
Statute, many deſperate Fellows
(that could read as Clarks) to
thoſe

thofe they had a mind to quarrel withal) would ufe all means to make them firike firft, and then fuddenly ftab them; and by this way avoid the faid Statute, and become · guilty only of a Man-flaughter at Common Law, and fo receive the benefit of Clergy, which the Statute takes away. The other Cafe was in the fame Circuit, very lately, before Mr. Juftice (*y*) *Windham*, at the Af-fizes at *Worcefter*, a little before his death, Where a Father cor-recting his Son, for fome undutiful-nefs he conceived in him (having a Knife in his hand, being eating his dinner) ftruck his Son over the back with his knife, and gave him a ftab whereof he died: The Judge apprehended this Offence to be within the Statute, notwith-ftanding that Exception in the Statute, of a Father correcting or chaftifing his Child or Servant, in regard it was an unreafonable way and means of correction: whereupon he reprieved the Fa-

(*y*) Sir *Wadham Windham*, Kt. one of the Ju-ftices of the Common Pleas.

O ther

ther for fome fhort time, and advifed with the reft of the Judges at *Serjeants Inn*, and after he had their Opinions that it was within the Statute, he forthwith fent down a Warrant to the Sheriff to do Execution, having received Judgment of Death at the Affizes; and yet the words of the faid Act of Parliament are (*although his Son, or Servant, dye of fuch correction, he fhall not be within the faid Act*).

Obferve here how neceffary it is, That all the circumftances that can be in an offence of blood, be put into an Indictment, and be fo found by the Grand Jury (as it is advifed by the King's Counfel) where there is innocent blood fhed by the party indicted, that every part and circumftance of the Fact, with all its aggravations, may come to be confidered and weighed by the Court, which otherwife cannot be; as in this Cafe of the Father killing his Son, if the Indictment had not been drawn up-

on

on the Statute, but at Common
Law, in regard of that Exception
in the Statute (as the Grand Jury then would have had it) the
party had been capable of Clergy,
and so might have escaped that
Judgment of Death. If such difficulties appear to the Learned
Judges, upon due consideration of
the Law, and of all circumstances
in cases of blood, how much more
will it prove difficult to Grand Jurors? and how little reason have
they to expunge, alter, and obli-
terate circumstances of aggravation in such an Indictment, upon
hearing only of one side, as they
please, and so prevent the Judgment of the Court therein, taking
from them the power, even to examine such a circumstance, as may
(if truly stated and examined)
rule the whole Case, as before is
observed.

    In all the Offences formerly
mentioned, where Clergy is taken away by those Statutes, there
is no new offence of Felony or Mur-

ther

ther made, that was not so before
the making of thoseLaws,as might
be inftanced in Murther, Robbery,
Burglary, Sacriledge, Cutting of
Purfes, Stealing of Horfes, Rape,
and the like; but only Clergy taken away from the Offender
(which is no more but the abufive
bloody liberty of Clerks in thofe
times reftrained) as wilful Murther where malice appeared, and
other mixt and fimple Felonies,
which were then moft raging and
reigning Offences in the Kingdom,
and cryed out for a greater Remedy, a ftricter Law to be made a-
gainft them (as appears by the
Preambles of thofe Statutes that
take away Clergy in thofe Special
Cafes) that were Murther and
Felony at the Common Law before; from whence I conclude,
that the Forms of Indictments of
(z) *the name of* Felony or (z) *Murther*, are no
Murther was
not changed,
but the Law alters continually for the heinousness of the Crime.
... not the same, then not the words that

way

way directed to be altered by
those Statutes that take away
Clergy, but are to continue in the
same form as they did before
at the Common Law. And I am
not of their Opinion, That the
words (*ex malitia præcogitata*)
came into Indictments immediately after the aforesaid Statute of
23 *H.* 8. Certainly there were
Murthers committed, and that frequently, of malice fore-thought,
before the making of that Statute,
and those Murtherers had their
Clergy also; otherwise that Statute
had never been made to take it
away. If the Grand Jurors shall
say, *They will not find those words*,
Ex malitia præcogitata, *put into the
Indictment, except the malice be
plainly proved to them* ; then fare-
wel that distinction and inference
of implied malice, which the Law
makes, in many Cases, and which
otherwise cannot be made ; they
may as well say, *That they will
not find such words Treason,
that are Treasonable, because no*

23 H. 8.

O 3   *Act*

Act of *Parliament*, or *express Case at Common Law*, *says those particular words are Treason*; or that they will find no Indictment of *Burglary*, although the Goods stoln be found with the Thief, and the dwelling House broke, because no Witness stood by to see the breaking of the House, entring into it, and stealing thence the Goods : Or against a Cut-purse, though the Purse or Mony be found in his hand, or because none see him take it forth of his Pocket; or to find the Indictment, because it is laid to be done Vi & armis, with force and arms, and yet said to be done (in the same Indictment, clam & secrete, & sine notitia) privily, secretly, and without notice of the party, which (in Fact) could not be done if it were done by force or arms: Or to find an Indictment of Robbery done upon the High-way, against those that rob in Vizards, notwithstanding the mony be owned, and found about them, because the

the party cannot fwear he faw their faces, and that thefe were the men: Or that fuch a one kill'd a man, that comes out laft from him with a bloody Sword in his hand, and no perfon befides with him. In all thefe Cafes it is poffible, the Parties accufed might find the Goods ftoln; and fo might the bloody Sword be found, and another do the Fact; but fure here is great and violent prefumption (fufficient for an Accufation) for a Grand Jury to find an Indictment (which is but an Accufation upon Record) to bring the Delinquent, or Party fo ftrongly fufpected, to a Judicial Trial; and as well may it be prefumed, when one Chriftian is kill'd by another, it may be Murther, that there may be a feed of malice in the will of him that did it, by a voluntary and fpontaneous motion in that act, that may. (upon a greater Debate) contain fome circumftance in it, that by fome reafon in Law (better known to the Learned Judge,

O 4 than

than the Grand Jurors) that may in Law prove malice expreffed or implyed in the criminous Perfon.

And if it be fo difficult in cafes of blood for Grand Jurors to determine what is Murther , and what is not, let them confider how dangerous a thing it is for them to mifcarry in their Prefentment in cafes of blood , of innocent blood (as is before manifefted) and fo acquit the Murtherer , and take the imputation of blood-guiltinefs with them, from the Affizes to their refpective Families, where it may and will cry againft them and the whole Kingdom for vengeance : I do therefore fubmit it to their ferious confideration , upon what hath been faid , Whether it be not much better, and a fafer way for them , to fubmit their Judgments herein to the Rule of Law , and the Refolutions of the Learned Judges, than by their extenuating prefentment (for the Court can go no higher than they pre-

prefent) to ftifle Juftice in the
birth, and to acquit a Murtherer:
For the Indictment, although no
part of the Trial, yet is the very
Bafis and Foundation of all the o-
ther Proceedings. And let them
confider how ftrict (formerly) the
very Law of *England* was in King
Edward the Second's time in cafes of blood, where the very will
and intent to kill a man (although
it was not executed) was punifhed for the Deed) although the
party wounded recovered of his
wounds.

A memorable Cafe there was
in that King's Reign, cited by
Juftice *Stamford*, where one com-
palled the death of another, and
did fo grievoufly wound him, that
he left him for dead, but afterwards the party reeovered; this
was then adjudged Murther, becaufe his will appeared fo plainly
to have kill'd him. For, as *Bracton* fays, *In maleficiis fpectatur
voluntas, & non exitus*, then was
the Will by our Law (as it is yet
:   be-

Stamf. fol. 17.
Pl. Coron. Tit.
Coron.Fitz.
V.15 Ed.2.p.
383.

before God) reputed for the Deed:
But now our Law couples the
Will and the Act together in cases
of blood ; but looks more upon
the Act than the Will : For though
the Will do neither intend the
Act (as it is done) nor approve
of it (after it is done) yet if the
Will in any part of the Act be criminous, it makes the Offender
(in our Law) in cases of blood,
guilty of the whole Fact, with all
the obliquity and evil in it.   As if
a man intend only to beat another,
to ftrike him, but not to kill him,
and the party die of the ftroke, it
may be murther in him that gave
the ftroke.   So if three men come
to make a Diffeifin, and one of
the three kill a man, the other
two perfons are guilty, as principals in the murther, although they
neither confent to it, will it, or
ftrike the Party, nor came with
that intent, but only were in company to have done another Act.
So if one, to kill his Wife, give her
(lying fick) Poyfon in a roafted
Apple,

Vid. Tit. Me-morat. p.331, 350.

Hales & Petit Cafe le Com. 261.a.

18 El. Pl.474.

Apple, and fhe eating a little of
it , give the reft to a little Child of
theirs , which the Husband (left
he fhould be fufpected) fuffereth
the Child to eat, who dieth of
the fame poyfon, this is murther
though the Wife recover ; for the
Poyfon miniftred upon malice prepenfed to one, which by a con-
tingency procureth the death of
another whom he meant not to
kill , nor bear any malice to ,
fhall be as great an Offence as if
it had taken the effect which he
meant, proceeding from a naugh-
ty and malicious intent. So where
two men combat together , upon
the evil and provoking words of a
woman , and the one killeth the
other , the woman in this cafe was
Arraigned of the death of him
that was kill'd ; and in this Cafe
the Grand Jurors found it murther So if an ignorant perfon
take upon him to give Phyfick to
one that is not well , and through
his ignorance adminiftreth that
unto him that (apparently) kills
him,

him, this is murther. And so
it might be inftanced in many fi-
milar Cafes, which are not to be
difputed by Grand Jurors, but
prefented by them *in re. forma*,
as the Indictment is advifed by
the King's Council, and comes to
their hands, where they find (as
before is faid) a criminous Party in the Indictment, and a Body (found) of a reafonable Creature, certainly, or probably kill'd
by him, although the Evidence
be not exprefs to every circumftance of aggravation, as it is
laid down in the Indictment,
whereby to bring the Party and
his Offence of Blood to a full
Trial by a fecond Jury, which
otherwife can never be done,
neither the Law therein known
from the Court in fuch a Cafe.

Befides, many other Inconveniences and doubts may arife where
the Grand Jury find the Bill of
Indictment only *Manflaughter*,
which by finding of it *Murther*
would be prevented, as in chal-
lenging

lenging upon his tryal above the number of twenty Jurors; the Statute of the 22 *H.8. c.*14. reduceth peremptory challenge upon an Indictment or Appeal, which at the Common Law was allowed to the Prifoner, to challenge thirty five Jurors (which is under the number of three Jurors;) this Statute fo provides, That *a Prifoner fhall not now in* Petit Treafon, Murther *and* Felony, *challenge above twenty Jurors, without fhewing caufe :* And in cafe of Treafon, and mifprifion of high Treafon, it was taken away by the Statute of 33 *H.* 8. but now by the Statute of 1, & 2 *Phil.* & *Mar.*the Common Law is revived, *for any Treafon the Prifoner fhall have his challenge to the number of* 35 ; and fo it was refolved by all the Juftices upon conference between them in the Cafe of Sir *Walter Rawleigh* and *Geo.Brooks:* By this Statute it is plain, that if one be Indicted or Appealed for *Murther,* and challenge above
                                    the

Marginal notes:

22 H.8. c.14. *made perpetual* by 32 H.8.3. Brook *Challenge* 217.

33 H. 8.

1,2 Ph.& Mar.

Hil. Ja. R.

the number of twenty Jurors peremptorily (without shewing
cause) it shall be a Conviction of
the offence and Capital; but it is a
great *quære*, whether he that is
Indicted or Appealed only for
Manslaughter (which is not named
in this Act, nor can be rationally
comprehended in the word *Felony*
more than Murther might have
been) may not challenge thirty
five Jurors, as at Common Law?
so it may be a *quære*, where the
Prisoner Indicted only of Manslaughter, shall stand mute, or will
not answer directly to the Indictment, whether notwithstanding he
shall not have his Clergy? for the
Statute of the 1 of *Ed.6.c.*12. and
other Statutes that take away
Clergy from such offences and Offenders (as are therein mentioned)
take it away as well from such as
stand mute, answer indirectly or
challenge peremptorily above the
number of twenty, as from those
that are convicted by Verdict, or
Confession upon their Arraignment;

ment; otherwife fuch as ftand Mute, anfwer indirectly, or challenge peremptorily, might have had their Clergy (as the Act feems to imply) otherwife it had not taken Clergy away in thofe cafes.

The Judgment of *Paine fort & dure*, that is, *Pain grievous and durable*, was not at the Common Law, but ordained by the Statute of *Weft.* 1. made *Anno 3 Ed.* 1. whereby it was enacted, That *notorious Felons, openly known of evil name, who will not put themfelves upon Enquefts of Felonies, which men do profecute at the Kings fuit, fhall be put in hard and ftrong Prifon, as they which refufe to be tried by the Law of the Realm; but this is not to be intended of Prifoners which be taken of light Sufpicion.* By which Statute it doth appear, that none fhall be judged to this pain, if there be not evident or probable matter to convince him of the offence whereof he is arraigned, or

Stamford *lib.2. fol.*149.
Pɔulton *De Pace, fol.*211.

or otherwife, that he is a notable Thief, or openly known to be of Evil name; which the Judge ought ftrictly to examine before he proceed to this Judgment againft him, it would be very hard (which the Law is never *in favorem vitæ*) to extend this Statute to *Manflaughter*, which may be fuddenly committed by one of good name and fame, and not a notorious Thief (as this Act mentions) and yet may have an obftinate humor to refufe Trial, challenge peremptorily, and make indirect Pleas.

It is the fevereft Judgment (that I know) the Law paffes upon any Offender, and therefore not to be extended further than the plain underftanding of the words of the Act, a Sentence fo fevere, that (I think) never *Englifh* man as yet (though many have been Preft to death) had the heart to execute it according to the letter, which Sentence is as followeth, That *the Prifoner fhall be fent to the Prifon from whence he*

he came, and put into a Mean 4 Ed.4.11.
houfe, ftopped from light, and there 14 Ed. 4.7.
fhall be laid upon the bare ground; 6 H.4.2.
without any Litter, Straw, or o-
ther covering, and without any
Garment about him; faving fome-
thing to cover his Privy members,
and that he fhall lie upon his back,
and his head fhall be covered; and
his feet bare, and that one of his
Arms fhall be drawn with a Cord
to one fide of the houfe, and the
other Arm to the other fide, and
that his Legs fhall be ufed in the
fame manner, and that upon his
Body fhall be laid fo much Iron and
Stone as he can bear, and more,
and that the firft day after he fhall
have three morfels of Barley-
bread, without any Drink, and No Forfeiture
the fecond day he fhall drink fo but of Goods.
much as he can, three times, of the Fit.Efch. 19.
Water which is next the Prifon-
door, faving Running-water, with-
out any Bread; and this fhall be
his Diet until he die.

P   Another

Another inconvenience may a-
rife, where the party Indicted and
Arraigned only of *Manflaughter*
fhall plead a Forrein plea of fome-
thing done in another County, to
the delay of Juftice ; the Statute
of the 22 *H*. 8. *c*. 14. only provi-
ding, in cafes of *Petit Treafon*,
Murther, or *Felony*, that Forrein
pleas in thofe Cafes fhall be tried
before the fame Juftices before
whom fuch perfons fhall be Arraigned, and by the fame Jurors
of the fame County that fhall trie
the petit Treafon, Murther, or

Coke 3 *Inft.*
fol. 27.

Felony. If a man be Indicted of
Treafon he may plead a Forrein
plea, which fhall be tried in another County, otherwife in cafes of
Murther, *Petit Treafon*, and *Felony*.

6 H.8.c.6.

Another inconvenience may be
upon the Statute of the 6 *H.8. c.6*.
By that Statute, the Juftices of the
Kings Bench are impower'd to remit the bodies of *Felons* and *Murtherers* removed thither to be
tried in the County, and their Indictments

dictments removed into that
Court, which before they could
not do by the Common Law; because a Record that is once
brought into the highest Court,
could not be remanded to an In-
ferior, *Stamf. fol.* 157. this Sta- Stamf.fol. 157.
tute only provides in case of
Felony and *Murther*, not *Manslaughter*.

The last Inconvenience I shall
mention (though I could many
more) by reason of Indictments
of *Manslaughter*, will be in Cities,
and Burroughs, and Corporations,
that have power to try *Murthers*
and *Felonies* ; the Statute of the
23 *H. 8. c.* 13. provides, That *in*   23 H.8.c.13.
Trials of Murthers *and* Felonies
*there proceedings shall not stay as
formerly, or be delaied by reason
of challenge of such Offenders,
for lack of sufficiency of Freehold, to the great hindrance of
Justice; but that if the Jurors
be worth in Monies and personal
Estate Forty pounds, they shall
not be challenged, but admitted.*
P 2   It

It will be a very extorted conftru-
ction that upon this Statute, and
the others -before fhall bring in
Every Man-flaughter is Felony, but not e converfo. Manflaughters under the word
Felonies, whatever practice is, or
hath been ufed to the contrary.
I conceive it fit to be better confidered, for it is not fufficient (in
all Cafes, much lefs in this) without, or againft a Rule and Act of
Parliament, to juftifie practice
by practice; this happily in the
end might prove a Common Thief
to be an honeft man.

Befides, obferve the penning of
other Statutes, and that will give
a clearer light to the underftanding of thefe; by the Statute made
27 H.8.c.25.   in the 27 of *H.8. c.25.* it was enacted, *That no perfon or perfons, of
what eftate or degree foever, fhall
have power or authority to pardon or remit any* Treafons, Murthers, Manflaughters, *or* Felonies,
whatfoever they be, &c. Here
you fee the Makers of this Law
mention the word and offence of
Manflaughter, in terminis, and
not

not leave it to be underſtood, or to be comprehended in the word other Felonies, though it is moſt comprehenſively ſaid, *or Felonies whatſoever they be.*

So the Statute made in the firſt and ſecond *Ph. & Mar. c.* 1 3. *That* 1,2 Ph.& Mar. *the Juſtices of the Peace (one* c.13. *being of the* Quorum *) when any Priſoner is brought before them for any* Manſlaughter *or* Felony, *before any Baitment or Mainpriſe, ſhall take the examination of the Priſoner, and Information of the Accuſer, and certifie it at the next Goal-delivery,* &c. Here you ſee *Manſlaughter* and *Felony* both expreſt, as neceſſary, ſeveral times in the Act.

So the Statute of the 23 *H.* 8. 23H.8.c.12. *c.* 12. that directs the manner of puniſhing of offences in the Kings Palace or Houſe, ſays, *All Trea-ſons, Miſpriſions of Treaſons, Murthers, Manſlaughters, and other malicious Strikings,*&c. and ſo divers other Acts of Parliament (as might be ſhewed) that make

P 3 or

Kel.fol.98.

or intend any provifion againft Manflaughters, do particularly name the word *Manflaughter*, and never leave it to be intended or included in the word *Felony*. It is true, that by a Commiffion granted to certain perfons to enquire of all Felonies, they may thereby take Indictments of Murther; though a Pardon of all Felonies will not avail him who hath committed Murther, in regard of the Statute made 13 *R.*2.1.

And the Commiffion of *Oyer* and *Terminer*, made to the Judges every Affizes, that enables them to enquire of all Offences, hath thefe exprefs words in it, *And of whatfoever* Murthers, Felonies, Manflaughters, Killings; not leaving Manflaughters to be intended by the general words of *Felonies* or *Killings*.

Many more Inconveniences might be fhewed, but thefe (with what hath been before fhewed) may be fufficient, until better reafons appear to fatisfie any under-

underftanding Grand Juror, to e-
fteem it much the better way to
find fuch Bills Murther, rather
than Manflaughter, there being
every way lefs inconvenience in
it, in relation to the Laws of the
Land (until by the wifdom of a
Parliament they are altered) and
much more of fatisfaction and
fafety to their own private Confciences, that ftand fo deeply engaged to difcover Blood-guilty
perfons, and to fupprefs and filence
the cries of Innocent blood, that
by our Laws (in the firft place)
cries to Grand Jurors for Vengeance againft the Murtherer and
Manflayer.

It now remains that two Objections be anfwered, that happily to fuch as do not well weigh
and confider them may feem to
be of fome force againft what hath
been herein faid to the contrary;
the one is, *The general liberty,
and conftant practice Grand Jurors have taken ever fince the
making of the faid Statute of the*

P 4   23 H.

23 H.8.c.1. *to find, as they please, either* Murther *or* Manslaughter; *not as the* Indictment *comes to their hands from the Kings Council, but as they apprehend the Evidence that is brought to them, taking upon themselves not only the sole Judgment of the Fact, and what the Law is that ariseth upon the said Fact, taking the Judgment of the Law therein from the Court (although they hear but one side) and putting in and putting out what they please in such Indictments, notwithstanding it appears to them the party Indicted is guilty of shedding* Innocent *blood, varying the species of Murther and Manslaughter as they please, until after Arraignment of the Prisoner it be too late to amend it, as I have often known.*

The other Objection is (and this seems to be of some weight and authority in Law against what hath been said) *That Mr. Justice* Stamford, *in his book of*

The

The Pleas of the Crown, *is of another opinion,* viz.*That a Grand Jury may find the Special matter in the Indictment ; that is to fay, that the Prifoner killed the other* fe defendendo, *or* per Infortunium, &c.' *which the party upon his Arraignment may either confefs, or eftrange himfelf from the fact, and plead,* Not guilty.

To the firft Objection, as to the *liberty and practice of Grand Jurors to the contrary fo long ufed,* I Anfwer, It hath been before in this Treatife fufficiently made out, the great Inconvenience and mif-chief, in Cafes of Blood, that is the confequence of fuch practice, and that being granted (as it can-not be denied) I fuppofe no wife man will think, that the long practice of fuch an Errour will juftifie it, or encourage the longer continuance of it, in the higheft Courts of Law and Juftice, and in fo high and tender an Offence as the difquifition of Blood is, although in Inferiour County Courts,

Courts, where (many times) are ignorant Judges, and mean Clerks; and in ordinary Offences this Maxime may hold good, that *Communis Error facit Jus*, that the common practice of an Error makes it the Law of the Court, and not convenient to be altered; yet I have never obferved that Maxime to take place in the higheft Courts of Juftice in this Kingdom, before the Judges of the Courts at *Weftminfter*, Juftices of Oyer and Terminer, Juftices of Goal-delivery, and Juftices of Affize, who fit not to practice, but to correct and deftroy Errors of all kinds, efpecially in Trials of mens Lives, in Cafes of Blood, and whoever fhall urge that Maxime againft what I have here faid, doth by that fufficiently grant, what I have here endeavoured to prove, *viz.* the errour and inconvenience of fuch practice, which ought no more to be continued, than a long cuftome, when it is found to be unreafonable;

but

but I shall never allow (neither
can it be proved) that there hath
been in this Kingdom such liberty
and practice, allowed and indulg-
ed by the Reverend and Learned
Judges to Grand Jurors , to find
and alter Indictments brought unto them in cases of Blood, as they
themselves please and judge convenient ; they being (as hath been
said befote) not the Judges, nor
the Triers , but Presenters of a
fact of Blood, fit for the Judgment
of the Jury of Life and Death,
who only are the proper Judges of
the Fact ; for none can be said to
be proper Judges of any Fact in
Controversie that hear but one
side , for Grand Jurors hear no
more , and therefore ought in
Law , Reason , and Conscience
(where they find a guilty person
that hath had his hands in Blood,
and unjustly taken away the Life
of another person) to leave it (as
an entire fact of Murther) to the
Trial and Verdict of the second
Jury to find the truth of the Fact
(upon

(upon hearing of both fides, and
receiving the Judgment of the
Court) in what fpecies or degree
of Murther it is, which likewife
if any doubt or point of Law a-
rife in the Cafe (as many times it
doth) they may find it fpecially
(which a Grand Jury cannot) and
thereupon receive the opinion of
all the Judges of *England* (*Murther* being the Genus of the feveral Species) and in common
acceptation, he is accounted a
Murtherer that kills any man, or
reafonable Creature unlawfully;
and the Commandment is, *Thou
fhalt do no Murther*, which certainly comprehends all unlawful
killing, otherwife that command
is not well tranflated from the
Text, *Non Occides*, *Thou fhalt
not Kill*; and in my own experience, for above forty and five
years in one Circuit, I have
very often known many Learned
Judges, fuch as Mr. Juftice *Do-
deridge*, the Lord Chief Baron
Davenport, Mr. Juftice *Jones*,
Mr.

Mr. Justice *Whitlock*, and many others, often rebuke and reject the Presentments of Grand Jurors, in Cases of Blood, and other Felonies, where they have either varied from their Evidence, or from the Law, the Judges before hand having received some light of the nature and testimony of the Fact, from the Informations and Examinations therein delivered into the Court by the Justices of the Peace and Coroners (a very good Rule for Judges to observe) and often either put it upon an open Evidence in Court (which is very inconvenient) or discharged them of. such a Bill, and bound the Witnesses over to the next Assizes (which is also very inconvenient) in regard Witnesses may die, or the Prisoner may die, and so the Forfeiture is lost, and the offence unpunished; and in Cases of Blood there will be too much opportunity given for compounding and making an Interest with the Prosecuter ·and Witnesses;

and

and in these modern times, since
the happy return of our moſt gracious Sovereign, King *CHARLES*.
the ſecond, I have known ſeveral
learned and pious Judges, ſome
ſince dead, others yet living, and
eminent upon the Bench in *Ox-
fordſhire* Circuit, Fine and Impri-
ſon ſeveral Grand Jurors for their
miſcarriage and miſdemeanour in
delivering in Bills of *Manſlaughter*
inſtead of Bills of *Murther*, againſt
the clear and poſitive directions
of the Court. And this may ſerve
for anſwer to the firſt Objection,
from the liberty and affected practice of Grand Jurors (in finding
of Bills in Caſes of Blood) according to their own humor and appre-
henſion to introduce a Law, that
therefore they may find them as
they pleaſe, notwithſtanding that
the Court adviſeth and directeth
the drawing of them *MUR-
THER*.
    To the ſecond Objection of Mr.
Juſtice *Stamford* (in the place before cited) where he ſaith, that
whereas

whereas the Statute of Glouc. c.9.
*saith, That he ought to put himself
in an Inqueft* de bono & malo,
this is only intended (faith he)
when he is Indicted of Murther
or Manſlaughter, *and not where in
the body of the Indictment, the
Special matter is found* (as if the
Grand Jury may find eſpecial Verdict) *of* per Infortunium, *or* ſe
defendendo, &c. I anſwer to this
Objection, Certainly Mr. Juſtice
Stamford (though a very Learned man) did well conſider this
matter, and his Opinion therein,
when he ſet it down; for he informs you not what ſhall become
of ſuch an Indictment, where only the Special matter is found by
the Grand Jury, whether the party may Traverſe it (for it is but a
Treſpaſs) or confeſs it, and ſo
have his Pardon of Courſe upon
ſuch confeſſion, and then the Judges
that are to make the Report or
Certificate of the nature of the
fact to the King in *Chancery*, muſt
Certifie like blind and deaf men,
that

that never faw or heard any thing
of the merit of the caufe, nor underftand any thing by evidence of
the nature and circumftance of the
Fact; like the Lay-zealot, muft
believe as the Prieft believes, pre-
ferring Obedience before Truth;
but fure no prudent and pious
Judge will make fuch a blind Certificate, in cafe of Blood.

Befides, whoever fhall judici-
oufly and impartially compare and
weigh the Statute of *Marlebridge*
and the Statute of *Gloucefter* together, and the reafons of the
Statute of *Gloucefter*, what mif-
chief it was made to prevent, and
confider but the nature of the
thing, will never be of his Opinion
in this particular, there is fo little
of reafon or true meaning of either
of thofe Statutes in it. The words of
the Statute of *Marlebr.* are thefe,
*Murther from henceforth fhall not
be judged before our Juftices,
where it is found Misfortune.* In
the time of this Statute, it feems,
there were two Juries, the Grand
Jury,

Jury, and the Jury of Life and Death, to prefent and try the Offences of Murther, otherwife the Juftices could not judge of it, they never paffing Judgment upon a Grand Juries prefentment; which, by the way, fhews, that it is left to the Judges(not the Grand Jury) upon the examination of the caufe in trial by the Jury of Life and Death, to judge of the nature and circumftances of Murther, and of what fpecies or degree it is. This Statute of *Marlebridge* did only declare a new Law, that where it was found *per Infortunium*, or *fe defendendo*, it fhould not be Felony and Murther as it was before that Statute; but that the party in fuch cafe fhould have (upon Certificate of the Juftices before whom he was tried) his Pardon of courfe; happily then, upon the Prefentment of the Grand Jury; which might be the occafion of this erroneous Opinion of this Learned Judge.

Q   Then

Then comes the Statute of *Glou-cester*, as if the other had not been truly underſtood, or at leaſt had not ſufficiently provided for offences of Blood, and in plain words (as before is mentioned) commands, *That he that kills a man by misfortune, or in his own defence, or in any other manner without Felony, ſhall be put in Priſon until the coming of the Juſtices in Eyre, or Juſtices of Goal-delivery, and ſhall put himſelf upon the* Country *for good and evil,* that is, *for life and death,* which cannot poſſibly be underſtood where the Grand Jury find it but *per Infortunium,* or *ſe defendendo,&c.*for that is not Felony, and ſo cannot be Arraigned thereupon, whereby to put himſelf *de bono & malo,* ſo as to bring the matter to Iſſue between him and the King; nor can the Judge in that caſe (as is ſaid before) make a true and right Certificate of the offence and matter of fact, which muſt be ſpecially and truly certified according to Law,

Law, whereby to procure a pardon, as that Statute exprefly requires. And if the party fhall plead *Not guilty* to that Special matter found by the Grand Jury, what can that fignifie (as before hath been fhewed) for the Jury that is charged with fuch Indictment, muft either find the party guilty in Special manner, as it was found before by the Grand Jury (and that makes too fpecially Verdicts;) or elfe generally *Not guilty*; if they find him guilty of the Special matter (as the Grand Jury found before them) and the Judge and Court fhall afterwards adjudge (as they may, having heard the Evidence) that *fuper totam materiam*, it is either Murther or Manflaughter; then no Judgment of Death or Clergy can be given upon that Indictment or Verdict, but all muft be tried over again, and a new Circuit of bufinefs upon a fecond Indictment of Murther or Manflaughter; and how dilatory and idle would this be at an Affizes, in courfe of Juftice, and in cafe of Blood.

If Judge *Stamford* were alive again (although a perfon of great Learning and Judgment) he would furely (with fome other Errors in that book) recant this; neither is it of any advantage to the Prifoner, to have it found Specially by the Grand Jury, for he can never plead either fuch an Acquittal or Conviction in Bar to an Indictment of Murther or Manflaughter in the fame cafe (as before is fhewed;) and whoever fhall read and well confider this feventh Chapter, written by Judge *Stamford*, in *The Pleas of the Crown*, wherein this Opinion is, efpecially towards the end of it, when he comes to obferve the Letter of the Statute of *Gloucefter*, and how the Certificate of fuch a Pardon of courfe fhall be obtained, muft of neceffity hold his firft Opinion in that Chapter (for the Special matter to be found in the Indictment) to be very inconfiderately expreffed

for

for the reasons aforesaid. And
why may not this Learned Judge
(for *humanum est Errare*) mistake
in this, as in some other Opinions
in that Book of his styled , *The
Pleas of the Crown*? for which he
is detected by the Lo.*Coke*, and o-
thers that followed him , who
standing upon his shoulders must
needs see farther, than he did or
could; As to instance in some
few :

As first, that Respit of Execu- Stamf.*fol.ult.6.*
tion (where a Woman is *privi-
ment enfent*) where a Woman
after Judgment pleads her Belly,
shall be granted only (*says he*) in
Felony : whereas it is grantable Coke 3 *Inst.*
both in high Treason and petit *fol.*18.
Treason.

A second is, That the year and Stamf. *Pl.Cor.*
the day after the Murther and Ho- 63.
micide committed, shall be ac- 26 Aff.p.52.
counted after the blow given, or
poyson administred : whereas it
ought to be accounted after the
death, for then the party was Coke 3 *Inst.*
murthered, and not after the stroke *fol.*53.
or

or poyſon given ; *Coke* lib.4.fol.41, 42. in *Heydon*'s Caſe.

A third obſerved by the Lord *Coke* (writing upon the Statute 8 *H.* 6. *c.* 12. which makes it Felony to ſteal away Records) upon theſe words in the ſaid Statute, *Their Procurers, Counſellors and Abettors* , ſaith this Act, *expreſly extendeth to Acceſſaries before* ,

v.3 & 4 Ph. & Mar. *Juſtice* Daliſon's *Rep.* *and leaveth Acceſſaries after to the conſtruction of Law* ; yet there may be Acceſſaries after the Fact , for whenſoever an offence is made a Felony by Act of Parliament, there ſhall be Acceſſaries to it , both before and after , as if it had been a Felony by the Common Law : And therefore, though this Act expreſſeth only Acceſſaries before, yet it taketh not away Acceſſaries after, but leaveth them to the Law, contrary to the Opi-

Stamf.*Pl.Cor.* 160. nion of Mr. Juſtice *Stamford.*

8 H.6. c.29. And again , by the Statute of the 8 *H.* 6. *c.* 29. Inſufficiency or want of Freehold , is no cauſe of Challenge to Aliens who are Impanelled

pannelled with Aliens, notwith-
ftanding Mr. Juftice *Stamford's* Stamf.Pl.Cor. 160.
Opinion, *Pl. Coron.* 160. for this
Statute faith, That *the Statute*
2 H. 5. c. 3. ſhall extend only to 2 H. 5.c.3.
Enquefts betwixt Denizen and
Denizen.

But enough (and perhaps too
much) hath been faid in mention-
ing the miftakes of that Reverend
and Learned Judge Sr. *William* Sr.W. Stam-
Stamford, in that Book of his ford, Kt.one of
termed *Placita Coronæ*, Pleas of the Juſtices of
the Crown, which it feems by the the Common Pleas.
Title of it hath been corrected,
amended, and enlarged, fince the
firft Impreffion of it; which I
have not urged in the leaft to de-
tract from the Learning and Honour of that great and learned
Judge, or from the value of that
Book, which notwithftanding there
may be a few miftakes found in it,
yet is of as high efteem as any
Book of the Law, extant upon
that Subject; but principally to
fhew, that he may as well erre in
his Opinion concerning Grand Jurors

rors finding the Special matter, as in thofe mentioned; and that no human Author, in the Law, or any other Science, is infallible; and that we muft be very careful how we ground any Law upon the bare Opinion of any one, or two per-fons (though of never fo great parts or efteem) whereby to ju-ftifie or maintain a great Inconve-nience in practice, efpecially in Cafes of Blood, as before hath been fhewn.

FINIS.

www.ingramcontent.com/pod-product-compliance
Lightning Source LLC
Chambersburg PA
CBHW030816020726
47499CB00006B/1947